CW01217820

Imperfect Stories

Marco André
ALL RIGHTS ARE RESERVED.

No permission is given for any part of this book to be reproduced, transmitted in any form or means; electronic or mechanical, stored in a retrieval system, photocopied, recorded, scanned, or otherwise. Any of these actions require the proper written permission of the author.

Juan Esteban Ortiz, Creative Director
Megan Polstra, Text Reviewer
Jesús Camilo Barros, Design Director
Moisés Rubiano, Illustrator and Graphic Designer

Creative Writer, Independent Publishing

Table Of Contents

- **7.** Preface
- **10.** Imperfect Stories
- **12.** A Life Of LEGO
- **16.** New Year, New Me
- **18.** Do You Need All The Answers Now?
- **20.** The Koln Concert Story
- **23.** The Marco From Google
- **25.** 3 Things I Wasn't Taught In School:
- **26.** Just 7 Words
- **27.** The Octopus
- **30.** The First Christmas In My 40's
- **32.** 10 Things I Underestimated About Working From Home
- **33.** Ralph Meet Ruth
- **36.** Kintsugi
- **38.** The First Vacation Of My 40's
- **40.** Inside Out
- **42.** What I Thought Networking Was:
- **43.** Gangsta-Canine-Pup-Rap-a-Rhyme...
- **45.** Finding A Job Is Hard
- **48.** The Koln Concert, Part 2
- **50.** A Double Feature
- **51.** Life Is Always Worth It
- **53.** On Reframing Success
- **55.** How Do I Find The Time To Write
- **58.** 17 Minutes Late For The Interview
- **60.** The Antonietas In Our Lives
- **61.** Busting Assumptions
- **62.** The End Of Our Story?
- **64.** Little Moments Build Up To Big Things
- **66.** Levelling Up
- **68.** Ping Pong
- **70.** The Unsung Patrik
- **71.** The Story Of HAPPY
- **72.** A Letter To My Nephew
- **74.** Order Of Importance
- **76.** How Ingrid Rolls
- **77.** A True Partner
- **78.** On The Bench
- **79.** The Life Of Doc Robbins

81.	Tejal, From The Shop
84.	That's Who Tara Is
86.	Looking Up By Looking Around
87.	A Deep Kindness
88.	Strength In Weakness
90.	Why Was His Finger Inside A Greek Yoghurt?
92.	The Greatest Gift Of All: Time
94.	A Mark That Lasts For Years
96.	Just Simon
97.	"I'm On It!"
99.	The One Who Taught Me To Be Stronger
101.	A Really Foolish Question
102.	The Letters Of Indra Nooyi
105.	Feeling Overwhelmed Right Now? Try This
107.	How Southwest Airlines Turned-Around
109.	If Only
110.	Toxic Positivity
111.	Nice And Kind Are Not The Same
113.	On Being Real
114.	Soft Is The New Strong
115.	Arrivals And Departures
118.	Mental Health Is… Health
119.	The Idea That Changed VIMEO's History
121.	Being Kind At Work
122.	We Aren't Tired Of A 'Corporate' World
123.	7 Ideas When Starting A New Job
125.	Try This
126.	"You Have Gaps On Your CV"
127.	The Berlin Bottle Man
130.	What Lasts A Lifetime?
131.	The Little Things
133.	If You Broke A Leg…
135.	No One Has It Figured Out
136.	"I'm Toast"
138.	"The Mean CFO"
140.	Help And Mental Health
141.	Fear Of Failure
142.	"What If…"?
143.	Labels
144.	What Is Company Culture After All
145.	7327 Days
146.	Being Goofy

147.	The Character I Want To Be
148.	She Only Had 1 Follower
150.	Perspective Is Everything
152.	How I Manage Thoughts
153.	The Story Of Gabriella
155.	20 Things I Wish I Knew
156.	What They Taught Me
158.	What Good Leaders Did For Me
159.	Tell Me More
161.	On Feeling Regret
162.	Mental Health At Work
164.	Just Take An Interest
166.	Who You Gonna Call?
167.	Does Failing Define Us?
169.	How LEGO Came Back Into My Life

Preface

"One day my life will be perfect.
On that day, I will rest."

How many times have you had this thought? And how many times have I?
When we see it written down like this, it sounds a bit crazy doesn't it?
Almost destined to fail.

That's because Perfection IS unreachable.
Yet, we live in the pursuit of it.

In doing so we become miserable. We compare ourselves with what we see in others.
By how perfect we think their lives, their moments, their... stories are.

When I started publishing Imperfect Stories, the most common reaction I got was:
"I didn't know others' lives were messy too. So other people are afraid, or screw up too?"

Life is messy. Unpredictable. Full of hopes and fears.
Ups and downs. Joyful wins, painful losses.
It's meant to be Imperfect.

Our life story.
Our Imperfect Stories.
They are what makes us... Us.

You're not meant to read this book cover to cover.
Or in any particular order.

Maybe one day you get home, thinking your life should be "as perfect as others".
Then you'll open a random page of Imperfect Stories, and realize there are so many others out there. Whose life is Imperfect more often than not.

That there are so many Imperfect Stories, that we know so little about.
But not anymore. Not anymore.

In this book, you will probably find weird punctuation and messy sentences.

Some stories you will love, others you will forget.
Isn't that exactly how life plays out?

Stories, chapters and words... so imperfect.
That will make us realize that maybe, just maybe.
We should all aim for Imperfection.

Comparison is the mother of all miseries.
Imperfection is what sets us to a better life.

May this book be incredibly Imperfect.

Like You.
Like Me.
Like Us.

Imperfect Stories

Imperfect Stories

Imperfect Stories?
Stories about Me.
I always chased perfection.
Whole. Flawless. Unbroken.

But that made me feel.
Inadequate. Incapable. Anxious.
All the time.

How can I be as special as them?
How can I be more than I am?
When will I be enough?

But perfection is never enough.
That's its very definition.

When I aim for perfection,
I set myself up for something
I will never achieve.

If I feel this... could you feel the same?

Stories about You.

How can You and I stop chasing perfection?
What's its Kryptonite?

My hypothesis is realizing that:
We. Are. All. Average.

The more we realise it,
the more content we can be.
The more we are ok in our skin.

That's the 'why' of Imperfect Stories
that You, and I, live daily.

Imperfect Stories.
Stories about Me.

Stories about You.

When we were scared, and no one saw it.
When we are job searching and it sucks.
When the world thinks we have it figured out.
But we don't.
No one does.

We chase Perfection,
so Imperfect Stories go untold.

That's why I wrote this book.

Imperfection is Real, Raw, True.
Imperfection is Me. And You.
Imperfection is... Us.

A Life Of LEGO

April 2018.
A busy London street.
A mere chance encounter.
There it was, the one and only…

Star Wars Millennium Falcon.
That day, LEGO came back into my life.

My story with LEGO began when
I was 3-years old, with the Farm set.
Then at 8, I got the Fire Station.
Hoses, walkie-talkies and all.
At 13, I graduated to Technic,
a mix of beams and gear wheels.

But at 14, LEGO disappeared from my life.
Until that day, when I had just turned 38.
That day, on that street, LEGO returned.
And it never left the building.

Now every time I build.
Everything is Awesome.
It usually goes like this:

I stare at the box for 1 minute.
I turn it around, shake it.
I shake it again.
Just in case.

I break the seals.
Ahh, I love this sound.
I lay out bags, instructions, and stickers.

I claim all the bowls in the flat as mine.
Sorry, sorting tools are everything.

Colour. Shape. Size.

I spread the first bag across the table.
And so it starts:

Pick. Brick. Click.

The sheer melody of it soothes me.
For hours. Even days.

Pick. Brick. Click.

And when it all comes together.
With that last brick.
I get that feeling:

I. Built. This.

Some say building LEGO is pointless.
That you are following a recipe.
That you build it to take it down.
That it is not productive.

I respect their opinion.
But I know what's in it for me.
When I build, I become a child again.

Outside expectations quickly disappear.
I can be nervous, happy, anxious, or tired.
I can follow instructions or experiment.
I can build it alone or with family.
I can go fast or go slow.

I. Created. This.

No one is watching.
It's just me, connecting with myself.
Even if only for a moment, I am at peace.
Surrounded by bricks…
It all clicks into place.

Pick. Brick. Click.

LEGO became my ritual of connection.
My bridge to simpler times.
A way to achieve peace.

LEGO and I found each other again.

And we will never part ways.

Pick. Brick. Click.

New Year, New Me

Me, Me, Me. It's all about Me.
No 2022 reflections or 2023 resolutions.
No past or future. Now I'm doing what I wish:

I wish to make fewer assumptions.
When in doubt, I'll just ask.
Assumptions are the mother of all screw-ups.

I wish to see situations less in black and white.
Everyone has their own struggles.
To see life in shades of grey brings peace.

I wish to figure out faster where I belong and
where I don't. Where I don't, I let go.
Where I do, I fight like hell for it.

I wish to be as disciplined in learning how to
rest, as I once was in learning how to work.
It's as equally or more important, not less.

I wish to let go of the past mistakes and
triggers that haunt me. I learned, I felt the pain.
Now I move on.

I wish to measure my decisions not by their
outcomes, but on how aligned they were with
my values.

I wish the things I 'have to do' for my mental
health stop being a thing. They're part of who
I am and how I live.

I wish to be as kind to myself as try to be to
others. To focus on changing me, instead of
seeking to change them.

Because If I don't sort my stuff out first.
How can I expect others to sort out theirs?

It's Now. It's Today and every day.
It's about Me, first.

Well, and my dog. I grant her an exception.
Because she's frickin' cute.

Do You Need All The Answers Now?

'I don't know what I want... but I want it now'.
Always pushing for the next thing.

My inability to be in the present moment.
Fueled by my fear of the future.

One day, I was telling my friend Wren.
About my anxieties for the future.
She interrupted me with a simple question:

'Marco, do you need to have all the answers now?'

I wanted to fight it. Argue back:
'Of course, I want all of the answers now!
How else shall I cope with this anxiety in my body?'

But I couldn't. She was right.
My crystal ball wouldn't prevent pain.
It would just prolong imaginary suffering.

Every time I now pick up my crystal ball and try to plan for 37 future scenarios, I ask myself this question again?

'Do I need to have all the answers now?'

Oh, it's not a silver bullet.
I still experience those feelings.

But. Everything. Slows. Down.
For a moment. Just a brief moment.

That moment gets me closer to living my life.
Closer to myself. Closer to the present.

In a world where I'm always seeking answers.
Who would figure that what would soothe me...
Was asking a simple question:

'Do I need to have all the answers now?'

The Koln Concert Story

At 26, I left my job and took on debt to study in Barcelona.

My mood was somber. The market was going down fast, as well as my chances to get a job fresh out of school in a downturn.
I couldn't get an interview, let alone an offer.

On that day, October 17th, 2008, everything was going wrong for me.

I had arrived home from a 14-hour day, with an exam and a paper to deliver the next morning. A typical student, I only had a frozen lasagna in the fridge.

I sat down, opened my laptop and... BAM. The electricity went out.

No problem - 'I still have my battery, a candle, and the neighbour's Wi-Fi (oops)'. But my battery was dead. Electricity was out in the whole neighbourhood.

I cried. I cursed. I thought 'screw you Universe, I'll call it a day'.
In resignation, I lit a candle and took a newspaper out. The title on page 13 (!) caught my attention - 'The Unique Magic of Keith Jarrett's Koln concert'.

For Keith Jarrett, everything had also gone wrong on January 24th, 1975.

He had not slept in two nights. The piano he ordered hadn't arrived in time. The one in the hall was a mess - the pedals didn't work, and the keys were sticky.

Keith was ready to cancel the concert.
That day would become a day to forget.

But at the last minute, he decided to play.

As an afterthought, the sound technician decided to record it. 'Just for the house archive', he thought.

When Keith played his first four notes 'tan din dun dun', the audience laughed. Keith was quoting the opera house's intermission bell. But quickly, as the concert pushed on, the laughter turned into awe and admiration.

Those 1,400 people witnessed what would become the most successful live solo jazz album of all time.

As Keith Jarrett's producer said afterwards, 'He played the way he did because it was not a good piano. Because he could not fall in love with it, he found another way to get the most out of it.'

I felt so close to how Keith had felt that night.
Keith hadn't slept in two nights. I wasn't going to sleep that night.
Keith had a substandard piano. I was left with a dead laptop.

Keith was a perfectionist. I was an insecure (trying to be) overachiever.

It took 4 hours for the power to come back on, but when it did, I put the frozen lasagna in the microwave and charged my laptop.

My outlook had changed. I cut that article out and put it in front of my desk. I pushed through the essay, the exam prep and a good-old cover letter for a job application.

To this day I keep a vinyl of the Koln concert, with the article cut out and neatly tucked inside the cover.

It serves as a reminder that things can always be turned around. Even if I start with those 4 intermission notes, I can make it work.

Those first notes given to me can be turned into a better tune. Every time.

'Tan din dun dun'.

The Marco From Google

For 10 years, I was known as the 'Marco from Google'.
So when I left, there was nothing. Emptiness.

At least that's how I felt.
Like I would never be as valuable.
Like I, the impostor, would be found out.
Like "Marco Andre, Incorporated" wasn't enough.

We become so enmeshed with the companies we work for.
Right or wrong, they become part of our identity.

When I made the decision to leave Google,
friends who had done the same said
it would feel like a break-up.

And it did. So how did I snap out of it?
I didn't.

I went back and talked, talked, talked.
With the same friends, co-workers I had known for 10 years.

They knew who "Marco Andre, Incorporated" was.
They built me back up. Brick by brick, chat by chat.

Until I realized that "Marco from Google".
Had shaped a part of what I had become.
But he wasn't WHO I was.

Breaking up hurts like hell.
But it allows us to put pieces back together from scratch.

And create something longer-lasting.
More future-proof.
More…You.

"You…Incorporated"

3 Things I Wasn't Taught In School:

1. Culture is defined by the behaviours you witness being rewarded.

2. Your title matters way less than the experiences and stories you can tell.

3. Your manager has the biggest impact on your physical and mental health at work.

Just 7 Words

He was always a man of great vision, and few words.
It was no different when he wrote my graduation message.
Scribbled with a felt-tip pen, at the top of a blue strip.
'With your creativity, you're gonna go far'.

7 words. Just 7 words.

Almost 20 years later,
those words still echo in my head.
And they continue to make all the difference.

Every time I neglect my creative side,
because it 'isn't professional'.
Every time I overuse the rational part of my brain (never know if it's left or right).
Every time I stop having faith in that part of myself.

Dear Professor Antonio Camara:
Thank you for the message you wrote me 20 years ago.
I'm still not where I want to be. But I'm on my journey.
And those 7 words make me try harder, every day.

Words matter.
Actions matter.
Gestures matter.

If you're working with someone,
write them 7 words today.
Or write them to yourself.
In 20 years, 7 words can make all the difference.

Just 7 words.

The Octopus

In the first year of the pandemic, anxiety, and depression increased by a massive 25% (WHO stats).

This means it's likely that one of us is now:
- Experiencing depression and/or anxiety
- Witnessing someone going through it
- Trying to educate ourselves on it

There are many challenges with depression & anxiety.

So why the picture of an Octopus plush toy?
Because one of those challenges is communicating what's going on.

For those of us going through it, we're so overpowered that we focus all our energy on dealing with it.
We are unable to even deal with what's happening, let alone explain it to others.

For those of us witnessing someone going through it, we feel powerless because we don't know what to do.
Our default is to ask about the cause, or offer different forms of help.

For us trying to educate ourselves, it can be puzzling and unknown.
We know that if someone breaks a leg, they put a cast on and rest until they recover.
But depression and anxiety are invisible illnesses, and more dangerous than breaking a leg.

Talking about it can at the very least educate us on an important topic... and, at best, one day save a life.

So how can we communicate better, and turn the invisible... visible?

For those experiencing it, focus all your effort on dealing with it. Try to replace the guilt of not being able to explain by imagining you had a physical injury. After all, no one would question you if you had a broken leg - the cause is easy to explain.

For those witnessing someone going through it, unsolicited small gestures mean a lot. Doing a chore, just being there. Signalling, instead of openly communicating how and why you are trying to help.

In our house, we have a simple reversible Octopus plush toy. We use it to signal how we are feeling that day, so the other knows how to adapt. If one is feeling down, we flip the octopus to his blue, sad face. If one is feeling good, the pink smiley octopus shows up. Simple and effective.

For those trying to learn about it - we can spread the word and talk to our kids, our friends, and our family. Help normalize it and break the stigma around it.

One day mental health won't be 'a thing'... it will just be.
We all have a role to play.

Including our very own Octopus.

The First Christmas In My 40's

So deep. So profound. Here are my 7 reflections
about the first Christmas holidays in my 40's.

As a kid, I loved watching Home Alone with my family.
In my 40's, I can't wait to be home alone without family. Just for 5 minutes, please.

As a kid, I craved going from dinner to opening gifts.
In my 40's, I'm so full, I can't move from the dinner table.

As a kid, I believed in Santa Claus.
In my 40's, I believe in dressing my dog as Santa Claus.

As a kid, I hated to be gifted scarves or socks.
In my 40's, I LOVE getting scarves and socks.

As a kid, I made mixed cassette tapes of Mariah Carey.
In my 40's, I read about Taylor Swift's feud with Spotify.

As a kid, I loved the fireworks outside at midnight.
In my 40's, I fall asleep inside before midnight.

As a kid, I had so much joy for every gift I received.
In my 40's, I get so much joy for every single gift I give.

10 Things I Underestimated About Working From Home

1. How Crocs and sweatpants magically match with every piece of my upper-body business attire.

2. How taking a 5-minute stroll outside, in the first hour of my morning, makes all the difference in my mood and outlook for the whole day.

3. How I am drawn to distractions I never found appealing, e.g. does my laundry really need to be done during business hours? Business rationale: you're more productive when the clothes you are not wearing aren't dirty. Makes sense.

4. How hard it is to have unscheduled focus time, because the only way to interact is not spontaneous chats anymore but meetings — and we crave that human connection. Proof: my exaggerated Pavlovian reaction every time I receive a sound notification — 'Is anybody out there?!'

5. How difficult it is to start a new job without having people around to ask all those 'stupid questions', such as 'What does that 3-letter acronym stand for again?'

6. How planning 'Who takes care of lunch' for the whole week on Sunday, dramatically changes the well-being of my relationship for the week.

7. How much daydreaming and talking to myself I would do… and how it doesn't feel like a symptom of something bad anymore.

8. How energizing it now feels when I do go to the office from time to time — like the first day of school after a summer break. The one opportunity I have to not say, "Can you see my screen now?" 17 times in one day.

9. How good is it to witness people in their home environments and hear their stories — and how this generates more authentic and meaningful connections.

10. How often I'd find myself listening to music without realizing it was on… and singing along at top volume without thinking twice about it — at least until my partner comes and knocks on the door, surprisingly annoyed.

Ralph Meet Ruth

Ralph meet Ruth, your partner for life.
The burger to your fries.
The Mario to your Luigi.

It started with a question from a friend.

My dear friend André Lapa asked me:
'Who's this person I sense hanging over your posts?
That calls you weak and soft?'

I answered: his name is Ralph.
He's the voice inside my head that tells me:
'You're not supposed to be here.'

Others call him different names.
Inner Critic. Impostor Syndrome.
I just call him Ralph.

He's been a tenant inside my head.
For years, for as long as I can remember.

And I can't kick him out.
At least I was never able to.
And believe me, I've tried. Many times.

This is what I do to co-exist with Ralph.

Getting him married.

Ralph, meet Ruth, your partner.
The Dusty Bun to your Suzie Poo.
The burger to your fries.
The Mario to your Luigi.

When you second-guess me, Ruth cheers me on.
When you make assumptions, she gives you facts.
When you scream at me, she whispers to me.
And raises her voice towards you.

We are in this together now, the 3 of us.
Living happily ever after.

Getting him out and onto paper.
The pen is mightier than the sword.
When Ralph's voice gets too loud.
I write down each thought or command.
Every stroke creates distance, perspective.
For a moment, I am Home Alone.

Getting on his nerves.

If Ralph says don't do it, I'll do it anyway.
A lighter version, but still do it.
I start small... and then watch how Ralph goes
from annoyed to (mildly) accepting.

A pitch for 50 people? I'll start with 10.
Writing a book? I start with an article.
The more I do it, the more Ruth says:
"It wasn't that bad Ralph, now was it?"

Ralph urged me not to write this book.
But I did, which kept him out of my head.
And wise Ruth told me:
'When others read it, maybe they will have a
break from their very own Ralph.'

So I wrote it anyway.

Kintsugi

Kintsugi. The Art of fixing broken pottery.
Turning it into something better than before.
This makes no sense to me. Here's why:

When I fell apart, all I wanted was to pick up the pieces.
And put them back to resemble the original.
The person I used to be wasn't there anymore.
I wanted that person back.
Truly, madly, deeply.

How can anything that was 'fixed'
possibly have more value or beauty?
How can embracing flaws and imperfections
make something more valuable?

Often I react this way to things I read.
I dismiss them or brush them aside.

My self-critic (Ralph) has a confirmation bias.
'Marco, disregard anything that DOES NOT
make you feel bad'.

10 good things from a career discussion.
I cling on to the one less positive one.

A good chat with a friend.
I focus on everything after the 'But'.

Back to Kintsugi - at first I was sceptical.
After all, being broken hurts like hell.
But then it dawned on me.
'Give more credit to a 400-year-old Art'
'Just give it a minute in your head'.

We were brought up with the idea
that being broken is bad,
that you failed yourself and others.

What if it is just the start of something new?

Something unique, strong, beautiful.
Even more valuable than before.
For yourself and others.

I was broken before, I will be again.
But I always have a choice.

Dwell in pain for who I used to be.
Or crack on (!) building who I will be next.
No pun intended.

The First Vacation Of My 40's

7 profound, deep insights from the first vacation in my 40's.

In my 20s, I spent my time at the beach playing beach tennis or cliff diving.
In my 40s, I absolutely DO NOT leave for the beach without my foldable armchair.

In my 20s, I spent all day on the sand and had a couple of ham sandwiches.
In my 40's, I come back home for lunch, cook a whole chicken and nap for 3 hours.

In my 20s, I loved playing in the pool doing splashy divebombs.
In my 40s, I stand by the pool silently cursing those who do splashy divebombs.

In my 20s, I woke up at 1 PM after a night out and went straight to the beach.
In my 40s, I arrive at the beach at 9 AM because I fell asleep on my couch at 9 PM.

In my 20s, I went to a music festival and stayed at the front, right by the speakers.
In my 40s, I stay as far back as I can, close to the burritos, bars and bathrooms.

In my 20s, I used tanning oil during peak sun time to get 'an even tan'.
In my 40s, 50+ sunscreen is my best friend and I look like a zebra on the beach.

In my 20s, every summer I wanted to meet new people.
In my 40s, I want to spend all the time with the friends I have for life.

If you're about to go, I wish you a great vacation!
And don't forget that foldable armchair.
It's a lifesaver.

Inside Out

Joy asked:
"Do You Ever Look at Someone and Wonder,
'What Is Going On Inside Their Head'?"
This is how one of my favourite movies starts.
Here's why it's so important to me.

In Inside Out, Riley is an 11-year old going through a life event - moving cities.
However, the main characters are the 5 emotions that live inside Riley's head, as she goes through life:

Fear.
Sadness.
Anger.
Disgust.
Joy.

What is brilliant about Inside Out is how it sheds light on mental health with joy, humour, playfulness and levity.

Fear.
"Alright, we did not die today! I'd call that an unqualified success."

Inside Out makes the heavy more bearable.
The complex simpler to understand.
The lonely less isolating.

Sadness.
"Crying helps me slow down and obsess over the weight of life's problems."

I wish Inside Out existed when I was a kid. When I had my own struggles inside my head. And I still do.

Even as a grown-up, I sometimes feel alone when I experience some emotions, thinking it only happens to me, not to others.

Anger.
"We should lock the door and scream that curse word we know. It's a good one!"

That's why talking about Mental Health is needed.
It's worth it to create an outlet for emotions.

It helps to know that this happens to others, that it's ok to have a hard time managing thoughts and emotions.
And it's ok when/if it happens to you.

Disgust.
"That's not brightly coloured.
Or shaped like a dinosaur.
Hold on - it's broccoli - bah"

It's never too early or too soon.
To spread the word about Mental Health.

With our kids, our parents.
With our teachers, our students.
With our managers, our teams.
With our partners, our friends.

And that's exactly what I'm gonna do today.

Joy.
"You can't focus on what's going wrong.
There's always a way to turn things around, to find the fun."

What I Thought Networking Was:

1. Getting power quickly through 'contacts'.
2. Attending events with a name tag poorly handwritten with my BIC pen.
3. Knowing who to call when I needed something.

What I learned about networking is:

1. Getting value TO others instead of FROM them.
2. Building a reputation for doing the right thing, especially when it's hard.
3. Forming one deep relationship instead of 100 shallow ones.

Don't network, create bonds.
Bonds last longer than 'contacts'.
Bonds go with you wherever you go.

Gangsta-Canine-Pup-Rap-a-Rhyme...

Here's a Gangsta-Canine-Pup-Rap-a-Rhyme...
Where I drop my anxieties as a new dog dad.
(Cue imaginary Beatbox)

Every day I try to be the best dog dad.
But inevitably one day.
I'll forget the poo bag.

Questions, questions.
Always on my mind.
Did she poop, did she wee?
Is that a tick or a flea?

Oh my god, her paws are wet.
Call them up now.
Let's run to the vet.

Questions, questions.
Always on my mind.
Did she rest, did she eat?
Did she play, did she sleep?

Too many, too many.
Toys for her to play.
But I'll still buy her one more, today.

Questions, questions.
Always on my mind.
How's my doggy, how's my girl?
Is my pup wagging her tail?

I know I shouldn't.
Give her one more treat.
But look at her, she's so damn sweet.

Pics of you, pics of us.
In my camera roll.

Lots of cuddles, lots of play.
I feel blessed, every day.

Questions. Questions.
Always on my mind.

(Beatbox. Over. BAM.)

Finding A Job Is Hard

Finding a job is one of the most isolating experiences
No matter if you're junior or senior, experienced or not.
We have all been there…. or are there now.
Like everyone else, what I felt during job hunting was:

1. Ashamed and alone at times.
2. Like nothing I did produced outcomes.
3. A rollercoaster of emotions.

But here's what I learned with time, with a little help from Gloria Gaynor.

1. I was not alone. Others had gone through the same, regardless of how successful they were. I was in the arena, there was nothing to be ashamed of.

Hell yeah, 'at first I was afraid, I was petrified'.

Then, with a little courage, I sent an email to friends:
Here I am, looking for a job. Here's what I'm looking for, and here's how I am asking you to help me.

'You think I'd crumble?'
'You think I'd lay down and die?'

2. I felt my outcomes were nothing compared to my strenuous efforts.

I did 100 things and only saw the result of one.
And it felt like it took 100x longer than it should have.

A friend once told me, 'trust the small wins, trust the process'.
I wanted to tell him: 'turn around now, you're not welcome anymore'. But I went with his advice instead.

'So I grew strong and I learned how to get along'.

3. I felt like me and work were breaking up daily.
If I was close to finding a job, I felt euphoric.
If bad stuff happened, my self-worth went down the drain.

So I learned to work hard, and rest intensely.
Without feeling guilty.

'I've got all my life to live'
'And I've got all my love to give'
If you're looking for a job and in a bit of a slump...
All I can say is: 'You will survive'.

One day your job will be back, 'from outer space'.
You will look at it in the face and think:
'Weren't you the one who tried to hurt me with goodbye?'
'You think I'd crumble?'
'You think I'd lay down and die?

'Oh no... not I. I will survive'.

The Koln Concert, Part 2

I couldn't get my head around it. What could have made Keith Jarrett change his mind at the last minute? What had led to this performance of a lifetime?

So I decided to dig into it and was amazed by what I found.

The story starts with Vera Brandes, a 17-year-old music producer. She wanted to bring together her passion for jazz and her love for her hometown, Cologne.

On that day, Jan 24th 1975, she woke up jazzed.

Keith Jarrett, a star musician, had accepted her invitation to play at Koln's Opera House.

But everything was going wrong that day.

The staff had brought the wrong piano - the baby piano used for rehearsals. When Keith saw it, he threatened to cancel the show. Vera couldn't find a replacement piano in a few hours.

So she pleaded with the sound technicians, 'please make it playable'.

Keith was in bad shape - after a long drive from Zurich, he had severe back pain. To distract Keith from the frustration, Vera booked a local restaurant for dinner.

But they mixed up his order… late for the show already, Keith only had time to take 2 mouthfuls.

'Jesus Christ, what else would happen that night?', Vera thought. She was about to find out.

Keith was done. 'A day to forget', he thought. He climbed into a taxi to head back to the hotel.

But Vera knocked on his window, absolutely drenched in rain. With a pleading gaze, she repeatedly asked him: 'Please play for the 1400 people waiting in the hall. They are here for you.'

Keith felt sorry for her. There she was, a little girl, at the start of her career. No one would judge him for giving up that night. But maybe Vera was the sign he needed to push through.
He finally said 'I will play for you. Never forget. Only for you.'

And so, he did. The rest is history.

At the end, witnessing a standing ovation, Vera couldn't believe it. That was not the outcome she had predicted earlier in the day. But she was proud.

I went back to that night in my flat, October 17th.
Why did I decide to push through?

I did it for my friends.
The ones I left back home to defy the odds stacked against me.
The ones that had unshakeable faith in me.
I imagined their faces smiling at me, saying in unison, 'You got this, Marco. You got this.'

Each time the thought of giving up came to me, I sat up straight, took a breath and repeated to myself:
'You got this, Marco. You got this'.

Find a reason - there's always one.
If it's something you really want, then push through.
Do it for others. Do it for yourself.
Do it like Vera. Or like Keith, find your 'Vera'.

What seems a 'day to forget', can be turned into a day to remember.
Just like the Koln concert.

Good or bad notes are coming your way, but you'll never know which until you play them.
So, do your best with the notes that are given to you.
You never know where they can take you.

A Double Feature

2 things that help me switch from pressure…
To joy and relaxation:

1. When I'm doing something 'unproductive', like watching a movie, I keep a notebook next to me.

If I feel guilty, antsy, or anxious, and thoughts like a task I forgot comes to mind, I just write it down.

I put pen to paper and let it lie there.

2. Taking on some form of focus work, preferably involving manual tasks.

Something where I can see a clear correlation between input and output - and see something taking shape.

My joy and relaxation ritual is building LEGO. But I have seen people going back to gardening, knitting, painting, or doing puzzles.

Life Is Always Worth It

Managing our Mental Health is frickin' hard.
To help me, I resort to the wisdom of others.
Nothing touched me more than 'Reasons to Stay Alive',
a book by Matt Haig.

There's a specific passage that I memorized.
On the hardest days, I say it out loud.

I know how it will feel after you read it.
I know it will feel unbelievable.
I know it will feel impossible.
I know it will feel distant.
I know.

But I often try to read it out loud,
even if sometimes I don't believe it.
Because sometimes to trick our mind.
We need to say it before we believe it.

The passage goes like this:

"You will one day experience joy that matches this pain.

You will cry euphoric tears at the Beach Boys. You will stare down at a baby's face as she lies asleep in your lap.

You will make great friends. You will eat delicious foods you haven't tried yet.

You will be able to look at a view from a high place... and not assess the likelihood of dying from falling.

There are books you haven't read yet that will enrich you. Films you will watch while eating extra-large buckets of popcorn.

And you will dance and laugh. And go for runs by the river. And have late-night conversations and laugh until it hurts.

Life is waiting for you.

You might be stuck here for a while.
But the world isn't going anywhere.
Hang on in there if you can.

Life is always worth it."

On Reframing Success

'What will be my next big career move?'
'How do I get my next promotion… tomorrow?'
'How do I get more budget, more scope, more responsibility?'

More, more, more. This is how I thought of my career.

When I thought about slowing down, I would be told off by the almighty judge in my head.

'But how can you think about letting go of what you have achieved?'
'You worked so hard, after all, the only way is UP!'
'How come you don't want MORE, more, more?'

Then I told the judge to shut up.

Because 'more, more, more' came at a cost:

Pushing myself to go from one career leap to another without resting.

Comparing myself only to those doing better than me.

Ignoring the signs of imbalance in other areas of my life.

Looking down on others that didn't see their career in the same way.

Postponing physical and mental fitness for 'when I had time'.

Missing out on opportunities to be with good people.

I try not to be hard on myself, this is how most of us were raised and wired to think.
At school. At home. At work.

But if we look at our personal lives… are they really that perfect? That linear?
Aren't they more of a wild ride full of ups and downs, starts and stops?

So why should our careers be any different?
Yes, this is how I was raised, but it's my duty to fight those biases and

assumptions.

It's ok to take a career break.
Because you want to rest.
Or spend time with your newborn.
Or learn new things.
Or just because.

It's ok to want to be a high-flyer or someone that 'cruises'. (What does that really mean anyway?)

It's ok to want to spend more time with your family.

Or prioritize your health. Or take interests outside of work.

It's ok to do all of these things.
What is not ok is... to constantly pressure ourselves or others to just go up, up, up.

Reframing success is being kinder to everyone, including ourselves.

How Do I Find The Time To Write

'How do you find the time to write?' a friend recently asked.
It was time to tell him my secret.

I wake up at 4 AM every day, after exactly 12.7 hours of sleep in a sustainable bamboo bed.

I slide into a 2-hour fire-breathing meditation, in which I break the time-space continuum to find inspiration to write.

I get into such a state of deep focus, that by lunchtime I write 2 stories, 1 autobiography, 3 romances, and half a children's book.

After slow-cooking a salmon I fished with my bare hands in a freezing river the day before, I have lunch while speed-reading 2 books simultaneously.

In the afternoon I have my daily meeting with my writing support team: my calligraphy instructor, storytelling coach, writing editor, and 2 friendly Umpa-Lupas that cater to each of my writing needs.

I finish the day by transcribing my stories into ancient Japanese characters, using a 14th-century Buddhist monk technique I learned in my yearly 5-month silent retreat.

Well...
Not really.

I spend my day like all of us, juggling life.
Doing meetings, emails.
Commuting, working.
Trying to keep all my plates spinning.
With no time for anything else.

So when I have an idea, I jot it down.
Then, I pick it up one day when I have time to develop it, at night or on the weekends.

Sometimes I write 200 words in one night.
Other times it takes me a week to write 500.

As easy as some make it seem, no one has it figured out.
That's why I admire fellow writers that bring their voices to the world, while juggling life.

Those who find the time they don't have.
To share their ideas, their craft.
Their voice, their art.

They are the real heroes.
The Imperfect Heroes.

Maybe we should all aim for Imperfection.
Comparison is the mother of all miseries.
Averageness is what sets us to a better life.

So 'how do I find the time to write'?

I don't.

17 Minutes Late For The Interview

It was 2011 - a candidate I was interviewing was 17 minutes late, and nowhere in sight.

On top of my high horse, I thought - 'so unprofessional, how can this be? Time to move on to the next candidate'.

Why do we set the bar so high when we're interviewing someone? Can we honestly say that these things have never happened to us on the job?

Life happens. It's as if we are wired to hold others to (impossible) standards, but we then expect others to be flexible with us.

'If he can't catch a typo on his CV, how will he deliver quality work if we hire him?'

'If she can't arrive at an interview on time, how will she show up for client meetings?'

Maybe he was trying to adapt his CV specifically for that company and role.

Maybe she planned to arrive one hour before the interview, but got stuck on public transport (nostalgia for the London Tube anyone?).

I too was guilty of this in the past.

Candidates had to be super-humans. Flawless.
But on that day, something made me pick up the phone and call the candidate:

'Hi, this is Marco - we were supposed to have an interview today'.

She apologized profusely, explained the situation, and interviewed in the afternoon.

Her name is Mónica Bagagem.
She went on to become one of the most competent and hard-working professionals I have ever worked with, with a brilliant international career.

I thought by 'allowing' her to interview I was giving her a chance.

It turned out I was the lucky one to get the chance to work with her.

The Antonietas In Our Lives

She showed up at the height of my lowest days.
'I'm just your cleaning lady,' she said.
Here's what she didn't know:

That when life was too hard to handle,
when my mind was playing tricks on me:

Your silent camaraderie made me feel less alone.
The lunch we shared mid-week gave me peace.
Your life stories provided me with perspective.
Your words of wisdom gave me solace.

And your damn good tiramisu gave me the best sugar high.

"My cleaning lady"...
You were and are so much more than that.

People like you, my dearest Antonieta.
You forget or we don't tell you enough.
That it's not about the job you have.
But the role you have in our lives.
The way you make us feel.
The mark you leave on us.
The hearts you touch.

Antonieta, even if you never read this, know this.
I miss you. But I am glad that others have you in their lives now.

How lucky was I? How lucky are they?
How lucky are we all to have you?
The 'Antonietas' in our lives.

I miss you, Antonieta.

Busting Assumptions

If we hadn't gone against 'what corporate told us to do'.
If we hadn't busted our assumptions open.
We would never have met.

Pierandrea Quarta was a brand manager at P&G, the client account I was managing at Google.

That day, he thought I was 'too busy to talk with a junior'.
I thought 'I was told to target only big guys, decision-makers.'

Yet, he asked if we could have a quick chat.
So we did.

That quick chat turned into a mutual partnership.
That partnership turned into a friendship for life.

And the thing is - he was already 'a big guy':

A brilliant marketer that took the brand to new heights.
An entrepreneur that left the comfort of corporate to found his own company - Rebo Bottle.
A friend that was with me in my darkest and happiest hours, with no judgement, without exception.

If we hadn't gone against our misconceptions,
look what we would have missed out on.

Assumptions are the mother of all screw-ups.
Making corporate more human starts by...
confronting our assumptions. And doing it our own way.

People over titles.
Bonds over contacts.
Questions over assumptions.
Relationships over transactions.

The End Of Our Story?

We hung up the phone.

We thought the same: 'Damm it. Can't believe we won't work together.' Was it already the end of this story?

I first met Gonçalo Gaiolas in 2020.

We went for lunch, and even before dessert, it was clear how aligned we were.

In our values.
Our thoughts.
Our views of the world.
Our passion for crème brûlée.

So we tried to find a way to work together. But at that time, there was no natural match, no simple fit.

We wanted it so much, but we were trying to fit a square peg into a round hole.

Until that phone call, when we realized it was just not the right moment.

From then on, despite living in different countries, we became close friends. And I learned so much with him:

How to be a leader that inspires others not by what he says, but by how he acts.

How to anchor on and protect what matters most - your close ones.

How to grill some damn good seabass.

And even how to mix growth, curiosity and self-care to become a better human.

Me and Gonçalo could've forced plan A, but it probably wouldn't have worked. And we would've missed out on plans B, C, all the way to Z.

That's why I'm glad we 'Let it Go'.

After that call, we thought we were burning our chance.
But we were actually lighting up the fire
of a friendship, that's gonna last for life.

Little Moments Build Up To Big Things

A global fun competition, the team wanted in. I said no - we had no time or resources. But their wisdom convinced me.

It was 2011 - Mónica Bagagem and Filipa Portugal Ramos had joined the team recently. We were working full-on.

No time to stop, to get distracted. I was stuck in my black-and-white views.

That's why I will never forget what they said:
"We will make use of what we have. And we will have fun with it along the way."

They grabbed a bunch of markers.
And used what they had, a big wall with the homepage of Google.

There was no creative agency.
No production. No brief.
Just our team.
Just us.

Fast forward to 1 month later and we won!
So I asked them - "what do you want to do with the prize money?"

When I thought they couldn't surprise me again, they said:

1. Use 90% of the money to build a micro-kitchen for the whole office to enjoy. A frickin' kitchen.

2. Use the rest to buy 3 bottles of wine and Madonna concert tickets (Yes this happened. And I don't regret it).

See, everyone screws up when they are a new manager.
I did and I still do.

And if someone claims they don't...
'YOU LIEEEEEEEEE'.

These 2 brilliant women taught me something then.

That little moments build up to big things.
That hard work can live with fun and laughter.
That wisdom doesn't come from what you know.
But from listening to what you don't.

Even if that means listening to Madonna's 'Like a Prayer'.

On repeat.

Levelling Up

As a kid, I loved playing video games.
I used to get stuck on the final level,
with the ultimate boss left to defeat.

I came across a boss-level mission last week.
Watching my dear colleague Iulia Serban.
During a 3-day, 20-hour workshop.
She was our master facilitator.
There she was:

Giving structure to keep us going.
But throwing it out when needed.

Calling out the elephant in the room.
Regardless of how big it was.

Feeling the room for what we needed.
Without us having to say a word.

Keeping us fair in each discussion.
Firing us up when we were low on fuel.

For 3. Whole. Frickin'. Days.

And the best thing is,
those who know Iulia know,
that's how she shows up.
Every. Single. Frickin. Time

Yet, she's not afraid of being imperfect.
She owns up to her mistakes.
She tells us when she's tired.
She asks for guidance when she's lost.

For me, those are the people we should look up to.
Those who inspire us without knowing.
The boss-levels who are humble.
The ninjas that sometimes trip.

The Imperfect Heroes.
Who are all around us.
Time to spot them.
Learn from them.
Spotlight them.
Cherish them.
Thank them.

So thank you, Iulia.
You're an Imperfect Hero we look up to.

Every. Single. Day.

Ping Pong

It was February 2011 and Manuel Román Cantón had just joined Google.

Our first meet & greet was by the ping pong table.
Of course.

Fighting his impostor syndrome, as if I was fighting my own, I told him:

'Manuel, I understand you. I feel the same.'
'But 10 interviewers believed you were up for it. It would be arrogant of you to think all of them were wrong.'

After I said it, he could've body slammed me against the ping-pong table.
I wouldn't have blamed him.
It was our first meeting after all.

But he didn't.
He turned his fear into preparation.
His anxiety into energy.
His doubt into drive.

A brilliant 10-year career at Google followed and he became a role model for many of us.

His ability to pivot from strategy to execution in the blink of an eye.

How he would act and speak, and the contagious passion he put into everything.

His vulnerability and realness in a time when being vulnerable was being weak.

And the way he always, always brought people along on his journey.

Today, he is the CMO of Netflix Spain and Portugal. More than that, he's a proud dad of 3, a great husband to Belen, a good human, and one of my closest friends.

I don't know if we would be close, hadn't we both dropped our armour that day. If we hadn't shared that moment together.

Of weakness.
Of insecurity.
Of humanity.

True connection does not happen,
when we're strong and shout about it.
But when we're weak and show it,
by bouncing back and forth.

Every day.
Every point.
Every game.

The Unsung Patrik

They slip under the radar.
Not the ones who made headlines with a grand feat,
or those who drew attention with a misdeed...

But the ones who shine day in and day out.
Like my colleague Patrik Kroslak.

Being a ninja at making the artificially complex seem effortlessly simple.

Focusing on what he can control, without getting bogged down by what he can't.

Connecting a hundred dots behind the scenes, smiling and carrying on even when we're lost.

Being easy to work with, building bridges instead of putting up walls.

Patrik, I know you shy away from the spotlight.
But not today my friend.
So thank you.

For being one of those Imperfect Heroes.
That are all around us. That teach us to be better.

Headlines and misdeeds are fleeting memories.
But Imperfect Heroes? They stay with us forever.

The Story Of HAPPY

I noticed the concierge's name tag: "HAPPY".

I had to ask: 'Excuse me, sir, is your name really Happy?'

He smiled, with a big grin, 'Yes, it is. My mother called me Happy. That's what she always wanted for me.'

I was intrigued. 'And are you happy, Happy?'

'Yes sir, I'm always happy', he replied.

I continued my line of questioning.
'So Happy, what is the secret to being happy?'

'It's simple. If I'm at peace in my heart…
I can deal with everything. Worries, troubles, problems.'

I was taken aback by his wisdom. 'It's good advice Happy.
But no one will believe me if one day I tell your story,' I said.

He grinned again. His trademark warm, gentle smile.
'Then let's take a picture, sir.' So we did.

I never saw Happy again.
But his words stayed with me.

Dear Happy, wherever you are now.
I hope, I truly hope you're still… happy.

A Letter To My Nephew

I wonder what would I tell my nephew.
If he is ever bullied at school.
So I wrote him a letter.

"My dearest Ed.

It's not your fault.

I know it's hard for you to believe me now.
I know you're thinking of 100 different ways, in which you could have avoided this.

I know that tomorrow or in the future,
you will say all kinds of things to yourself.

You will say that you should have put boundaries,
been fiercer, spoke louder.
You will feel the burden and unfairness of it all.

You will form a crystal ball that always predicts catastrophes.

You will be annoyed with your triggers.
You will be scanning for threats,
and discounting positives, because
that's what happened on your school playground.

You will be angry and feel powerless.
You will be angry about being angry.
All the time.

Your mind will trick you,
suggesting that acting differently
would've made a difference.
It probably wouldn't.
Because it wasn't your fault.

I know it sucks right now buddy.
But believe me, you'll be ok.
Just keep going.

One day you will be so proud of yourself.
As proud as I am of you today.

You'll be proud of standing up for yourself.
You'll realize that being you was enough.
You'll know this didn't happen because you were weak.
But because you were strong.

You'll accept that a bunch of heavy
stones were added to your life-bag.
Those stones were heavy but, with time,
they became easier to carry.
You used them to build the great human you became.

I know some days those stones will feel too heavy.
And you will stumble and fall.
It happens to me too.
That's why I know.

In those moments, I will lift you up,
put you on top of my shoulders,
carry that burden with you.
Even if just for one moment.

And, in that moment, I will say to you.
What I couldn't say to myself,
when I was You.

'It isn't your fault.
It wasn't your fault'.

Order Of Importance

He contacted me in 5 hours. I wasn't that important, just a prospective candidate. Still, he gave me the VIP treatment.

Summer of 2020. I was job hunting when I first met Jamaal Sebastian-Barnes.

Now you have heard me say this before - job searching sucks. It's one of the most enriching but also lonely experiences.

Doesn't matter if you're junior, senior, young or older.

When we're on the cusp of it,
a gesture that doesn't mean much to someone else,
can mean the world to us.

Jamaal's gesture that day made all the difference in my coming to Novartis.

2 years after, only now do I realize that I never got the VIP treatment.

That's just how Jamaal operates.

His measure of importance is 'What you need?' No matter how senior or junior.

He first seeks to understand, really. Only then to be understood.

He surrounds himself with great people.
Because without them, he is 'only' good.

If things are shaky for him personally, we can't see it.
He's such a rock for others.

He is far from perfect though.

He was a terrible influence on me,
in deciding to become a dog dad.
He can do more burpees in a day... than I can in a month.

Jamaal, may we all follow your example.

Treating the unknown as important.
Leading with empathy and heart.
Right when it matters.
Right from the start.

How Ingrid Rolls

'Here comes the new guy, wanting to change things. I'll put him in his place'.

She could have thought that… But she didn't.

That's not how Ingrid Tomkowitz rolls.
We started working together this year and she has been nothing but welcoming to me, the 'new guy'.

In her 30 years of experience, she has seen a lot.
But this doesn't stop her:
From choosing possibility over objection.
From choosing listening over judging.
From being curious to learn more.

When there's something new, she leads with curiosity and questions, not statements.

When something is against her values, she speaks up. With kindness and clarity.

When you go for a chat with her, you leave with knowledge, wisdom, and more.

When you can't figure it out. You call Ingrid, she'll help you out.

She knows she isn't perfect.

She's aware of how her stylish outfits overshadow my fashion choices.

She also shamelessly admits to copying the style of my Harry Potter glasses. Word.

So, thank you, Ingrid.

May we continue to be
lucky enough to keep you,
smart enough to learn from you,
and wise enough to want to be like you.

A True Partner

A true partner 'is a champion and a challenger'.
More of those empty corporate buzzwords.
What does that even mean?

My hypothesis is... being like Radovan Sahánek.

I started to work with him 1 year ago when he was part of our internal consulting team. And oh boy, how I witnessed him being a true partner for us:

Turning our thoughts into little pieces, pieces into a big puzzle.

Connecting the dots between us, so we move aligned, not estranged.

Showing us that we don't know... what we don't know.

Challenging our assumptions kindly, firmly, calmly.

Corporate buzzwords lose emptiness in the face of examples. And you're an example for us Rado.

A true partner - a champion and a challenger.
Keeping our perspective on track.
While always having our back.

On The Bench

It started in absolute silence.
On a little garden bench, 12 years ago.
When I finally stopped crying, she said:

'I could tell you 10 reasons why you're wrong.
But I'll just sit here in silence next to you.
I think that's what you need right now.'

Joana Santos and I became friends that day.
Exactly 12 years ago, on that little garden bench.
During those years, I learned so much with her:

That hard work, grit and perseverance.
Beat the crap out of 'Where did you come from?'

That doing the hard work on yourself pays off.
For you, and for those around you.

That you inspire not by being the loudest in the room at times, but by being the wisest, consistently.

That ultimate kindness is not about grandiose gestures.
It's about the little things.

It's about just being there, even if in complete silence.
It's about having a kind word, even if you disagree.
It's about cracking a joke, even if facing tragedy.

So, thank you, Joana.
From a brief moment on that little bench.
To a big friendship that will last a lifetime.

The Life Of Doc Robbins

Imperfect Heroes have superpowers.
One is bringing us Back to The Future.
That's what Doc Brian Robbins does...

I've never met anyone quite like him.
It's like 6 brilliant minds live inside his brain.

An always-on Student.
A steadfast Friend.
A dog Whisperer.
A witty Brit.
A Scientist.
A Psychic.

Before refuting anything, he first listens.
And then leads with curiosity, candour, and care.

He doesn't show off how smart he is.
He instead elevates us, without us even noticing.

He creates awe and admiration, not by giving the right answers, but by asking the right questions.

He treats everyone equally, respectfully. Regardless of title, rank or background.

By explaining to us the 'Why' of the past and the 'What' of the present. He shows us 'How' the Future looks like.

He's also Imperfect.
I say this objectively, overwhelmingly supported by the pure facts stated below:

His sarcasm is way better than mine.
His dog does more tricks than mine.
His fitness level outranks mine.

So thank you Doc Robbins.
As Doc Emmett Brown famously said in Back to The Future - this is a direct

quote:

"Roads… Where we're going, we don't need roads. We just need… Doc Robbins".

Tejal, From The Shop

I never fully understood her until that day.
I knew she was a great leader and human.
But I couldn't have guessed her backstory…

On that day, Tejal Vishalpura was introducing herself on a group call.

She told us that, when she was 16, she was working at a pharmacy shop.

Every day she was at that counter.
She witnessed patients struggling.
How healthcare could make or break lives.
How difficult it was for them to access care.

One day, little Tejal from the shop thought:
'Behind this counter, I can't help much.
But one day, I'm gonna help these people.
I'm going to go into healthcare.
And change this. I will.'

Fast forward to today, she built a brilliant career in Healthcare.

But more than that, she leads by example. And this is why we follow her:

She dares to challenge the status quo, and has your back when you do the same.

She elevates the ones around her, first taking care of others. Only then of herself.

She holds you true to your values, and inspires you to bring your whole self to work.

She makes us feel 'we are working for each other', because 'Together is Better'.

That's who she is.

Daring. Caring. Inspiring.

So, thank you, Tejal.

In your mind, you're 'just a normal person, doing their job'.

For all of us, you're a one-of-a-kind leader.

And for me, 'you're still, you're still'
'Tejal, from the shop'

Daring. Caring. Inspiring.

That's Who Tara Is

In an 8 AM team call, a new dad said: 'I'll keep my camera off as my son is still with me'.

We all thought the same, but she was the one that came forward and said:

'It's ok - turn your camera on, we want to meet him. My daughter is also here. Come on,' said Tara Roper.

So he did. We smiled, said hi to his son, and the (virtual) room was filled with joy and laughter.

What a beautiful, unique moment.
Of calm, levity and playfulness.

This was not the first time I saw Tara in action. When I notice moments like these...

Once...it's a gesture.
Twice, it's a pattern.
Over and over - it's who they are.

And that's just who Tara is.

When there's a difficult topic in the room, she introduces it. Focusing on people, leading with care.

When she doesn't know something, she asks. Without shame, but with curiosity and consideration.

Even if she's boiling inside, we can't tell. She's a combo of tremendous energy but at the same time calm, cool, and collected.

When something new or disruptive shows up, she's the first one to say: ' I'm on board, let's try it'.

That's why teams thrive around her.
Other leaders learn from her.
And peers admire her.

Despite this, she's not perfect.

Her comebacks to my jokes leave a severe burn on my skin.

And she recently went back to the UK, leaving a hole in the heart of her Swiss-based colleagues.

So, thank you, Tara.
For being one of those Imperfect Heroes.
Who are all around us.

That inspire us.
That we learn from.
That teach us to be better.

Looking Up By Looking Around

I used to look up for leaders to follow.
But what I learned with Aparna Vadlamudi.
Is that by looking around, I'm looking up.

I have been working with Aparna for 1 year.
And every day, I've been blown away.

By her kindness, her grit.
Her strength, her wit.
Her knowledge, her passion.
Her wisdom, her compassion.

She's fast enough to go at light speed.
But she finds a pace to bring others along.

Even if she's busy with a thousand things,
she finds time to check on me and others.

She's so smart in understanding complexity,
and she turns it into simplicity and clarity.

She outpaces us with her knowledge,
but she chooses to always be learning.

When she has all the reasons to be angry,
she leads with patience, with understanding.

Aparna is way more than a team member.
She's an example to follow.
A friend to be thankful for.
A leader to cherish.

So, thank you, Aparna.
I'm watching, and others are too.

And we're all looking up to you.

A Deep Kindness

'How are you? You look great today'.
He said in the elevator, with a big smile.
When we got out we asked him:
'Paul, do you know that person?'

He answered: 'No, but I felt like saying it.'
And that's how Paul Kinehan rolls.

In my career, I've missed a ton of opportunities
to appreciate those working alongside me.
People like my dear colleague Paul, who:

1. Make us smile with self-deprecating, witty jokes.
Normally involving his hair.
2. Bring us croissants and calorie bombs.
3. Often name the elephant in the room.
4. Always look for ways to help others.
5. Are simply unafraid to work hard.
6. Are never unkind to us or others.
7. Cheerful and smiley, everyday.
8. Only rarely get on my nerves.

If you have a Paul Kinehan in your life.
Write them a thank you note today.

I know Paul's kindness, he will deflect it.
But he is entirely worthy of it. Every day.

And if I know you well, Paul:
You will read this and say: 'Crikey'.
And then proceed to call me names.

Strength In Weakness

We spot heroes when they're at their best.
When they save the day, slay the dragon.
That's not what I learned with Helio Fujita.

I learned the most when I saw him, as our leader, going through hard moments.

How he handled himself in the defeats, rather than in the victories.

With him, I learned that realness is telling the truth,
regardless if it's a yes, a no, or a simple… 'I don't know'.

I learned that speaking plainly and simply is a sign of strength and confidence.

That you can be recognized, not by what you've achieved, but by how you got there.

That, even if you're in distress, you first take care of others, then yourself.

I learned that it's ok to share personal moments, they're part of who we are.

That if someone is in fear or doubt, we start by asking them Helio's signature question: "What do you need right now?"

That gratitude and appreciation don't need to be 'a thing',
they just come naturally, when there's trust and respect.

And finally, I learned that we should share the burden of defeats. And let others take the credit for the victories.

So, thank you, Helio.
For being one of those Imperfect Heroes.
Who are all around us.

That inspire us.
That we learn from.
That teach us to be better.

With you, I learned to set the bar.
Not at how I behave in the best moments,
but how I handle myself in the worst ones.

If that's not what defines a true leader.
Then 'I don't know' what does.

Why Was His Finger Inside A Greek Yoghurt?

September 2015.
The first time he spoke in front of us.
In his right hand, a Stabilo Boss marker.
In his left one, an open Greek yoghurt…
A frickin' yoghurt…

I had joined Pedro Pina's team and we had come together for a leadership offsite.

At that moment, Pedro's backdrop was composed of 2 pictures:

A breathtaking waterfall to the left.
An immaculate still lake to the right.

He was telling us about a quote from Wisdom, by Andrew Zuckerman:
'We spend so much energy in our lives telling the waterfall - stop, stop, stop, please be a still lake. When instead we should accept our lives are a waterfall… and let it flow.'

But why the yoghurt, you might ask?
Pedro had burned his fingers while making his morning coffee.
He was urged to seek treatment, but his team was together.
He wanted to push through.

So he grabbed a Greek yoghurt and dipped his fingers in, which he believed helped calm skin burns (please don't try this at home kids!).

It was a simple thing but it stuck with me.
If I asked him about it today, he wouldn't even remember it.
There was our leader, speaking about going with the flow, and walking the talk.

Those who've known Pedro for a long time, know he's an outstanding leader and friend.
But I didn't know back then, and that simple detail made all the difference.

See, I thought leadership was about…

The profound statements.
The grandiose gestures.
The bold intentions.

But making leadership human is about one thing: simplicity.

Simple words matter.
Simple actions matter.
Simple gestures matter.

Even if they involve Greek yoghurt.

The Greatest Gift Of All: Time

As she rummaged fiercely through each bucket, Tony asked:
'What are you looking for?!'
'I need to find it, it's not perfect yet', said Claire.

What was she missing?

The WHO: Our neighbours Tony & Claire.
The WHY: They wanted to thank us for watering the plants in their absence.
The WHERE: LEGO store, New York.
The WHAT: Minifigure Factory, where you can build your personalized LEGO minifigs.

Claire wanted to find the pieces she felt were unique to us.
She knew I was a recent dog dad.
So she didn't stop until she found a bone.

At a certain point, Tony calmly put a hand on her shoulder:
'Honey, you're going through another kid's bucket, his mom doesn't look pleased'

They didn't have to buy us anything.
Or they could have chosen something quick. Flowers.
An 'I LOVE NY' shirt.
Or chocolate. Lindt Hazelnut 22% Cocoa (generally speaking).

But they didn't.
Yet they gave us the greatest gift of all: their time.

The time to make it personal.
The time to make it caring.
The time to make it memorable.

I too default to throwing money at gifts.
I tell myself I don't have the time.
Or I don't have the energy.
Or I need to give something BIG.

But if time is our most scarce resource,
the one we never get back.

Isn't giving time the utmost act of appreciation and care?
Isn't it about the little things, born through the gift of time?
It's those little things.
That we treasure.
That we talk about.
That we remember.
That we carry with us.

So, thank you, Tony and Claire.
For the amazing mini-figures.
For these little things.
And for gifting us your time.
Because that was certainly…
No little thing.

A Mark That Lasts For Years

Some people you only know for days.
Leave a mark that lasts for years.
Jerh Collins was 29 years in the company.
30 days of which he was my manager.
But his legacy will live on. Why?

I only know what I witnessed.
I can only tell what I heard.

I witnessed courage. Betting on someone like me, for a job I had never done.

I witnessed kindness. Sending someone flowers for her 5 years at the company.

I witnessed realness. Simple thoughts, real words, concrete actions.

I witnessed leadership. Till his last day, ensuring his people were taken care of.

Now if I witnessed this in a few days.
What have others seen in 29 years?
Which stories would they have to tell?

I can only tell what I heard.

I heard that he always knew his team members' names, regardless of hierarchy, role or background.

I heard that when the going got tough, he lived by and stuck to his values.

I heard that he raised others up, standing at their side if they stumbled and fell.

And I heard that when he said he was leaving, several cried, but none rejoiced.

Despite all of the above.
He admits he's far from perfect.

He is open about his mistakes.
He is afraid of letting others down.
And he refuses to wear Crocs (why?!).

So, thank you, Jerh Collins.
Please continue writing your story.
And sharing it with 'We, lucky few'.

1 month of teaching for me,
29 years as an example to lucky others.
And a legacy that will last for a lifetime.

Just Simon

'Why weren't we brave enough to wear shorts at work today?'
Then he arrived. Sporting a pink polo, and bright green shorts. And said...

'Hey guys, you look a bit hot in those jeans don't ya'?
We all burst into laughter.

If I didn't know Simon Bestford, I would have been surprised by the outfit and the remark.

But I wasn't. There was so much of Simon in that moment, in how I always saw him act.

Someone that role models bringing your whole self to work, instead of preaching about it.

A colleague that does the right thing and stands by his values, even when it's hard.

A manager that is steady for his team, especially when things get shaky.

And a leader that doesn't need a suit or armour to be respected, to be valued.

He is far from perfect.

His outfits are way better colour-coordinated than mine.
And the way he pronounces 'stracciatella' is a frequent topic of heated debate between us.

So, thank you, Simon.
May we continue to have you with us.
Teaching us that laughter and levity at work.
Are not what we should shy away from.

But what makes us human.
What makes us whole.
What makes us...
Us.

"I'm On It!"

'Emre, I'm stuck. I don't know how to sort this out'.
He replied, 'I'm on it. Leave it with me'.
It wasn't even his job.
But he did it anyway. Why?

This is how Emre Düsmez rolls.

I was in the company for 2 months.
I had no internal network.
The issue was far from straightforward.
And I was about to lose key talent.

He stepped in and BAM - sorted.
That's who he is, how he operates.

Maybe it's because he's done every HR role known to man. Or he's simply putting his values and ethos to work.

Whatever it is, I know this.
Emre is the very definition
of a Partner to the Business.

He's a champion when needed.
A challenger when necessary.

When we are lost for words or actions.
He knows who to call.

When we sometimes lose patience.
He always keeps his cool.

When we can't bring people together.
He does it with simplicity and ease.

When we praise the calibre of his work.
He says 'I'm just doing my job'.

And when the mood becomes somber,
he lifts us all up, with a good dose of humour.

...and a hefty portion of the best baklava in the world.

So, thank you, Emre.
We were watching.
And we will continue to.
For many years to come.

The One Who Taught Me To Be Stronger

When she told me, it felt like a Mike Tyson punch to the stomach.
With an ear-bite.

This was my first thought. No idea why...
'It's Becky Thalmann
She's gonna push through.
She will make it.'

A few days after we got the news.
Becky, Lucia and I made a pact.
Complete with a calendar invite.

We would meet exactly one year later.
And from then on, every year,
wherever we are in the world.

To celebrate that Becky won that battle.
To celebrate our friendship.
To celebrate life.

Nothing prepares you for seeing a friend going through a life-threatening illness.

It teaches us how fragile everything is.

But as I saw Becky going through it, she taught me so much more than that:

That discipline matters, taught to me when I saw her at the gym after chemo.

That there's no shame in resting or asking for help from others, when/if we need it.

That inner strength carries you and those around you, without dropping a single ball.

And that in the middle of tragedy, there's space for love, laughter and levity.

For some, she is a survivor.
For herself, she aspires to be a thriver.
For me, she will always be Becky.

Not the person that survived.
But the one who taught me to be stronger.
Especially when things get hard.

So, thank you, Becky.
For being one of those Imperfect Heroes
Who are all around us.

That inspire us.
That we learn from.
That teach us to be better.

A Really Foolish Question

Someone I admire always asked this in technical meetings:
'I'm going to ask a really foolish question now...'

He did it thoughtfully and with a sense of humour.
The question wasn't foolish.
It was what I was thinking but was too afraid to ask.

I, however, was too afraid to ask because I thought asking questions was:
1. Not knowing my stuff.
2. Being weak.
3. Showing others the impostor I was.

Throughout my career, I witnessed examples like this one from my dear, brilliant friend Theo Fernandes. And this changed my outlook.

Asking questions really is:
1. Being humble - there's always so much to learn from others.
2. Being strong and confident.
3. Confronting that damn impostor voice inside my head.

"The man who asks a question is a fool for a minute, the man who does not ask is a fool for life"
Confucious

The Letters Of Indra Nooyi

When Indra Nooyi became CEO of PepsiCo.
She didn't kick off with a grandiose speech,
or a wonderful slide deck.

Instead, she chose to write letters…
to her employee's parents.

Let's rewind to October 2006.
Indra was at her mother's place in India.
Her mother asked her to dress formally and sit with her in the living room.

When visitors arrived, they congratulated Indra first.
And then her mother.
'You did such a good job raising your daughter. She brought so much pride to the family, and joy to the country'.

Witnessing this, Indra had an insight. 'When you turn 18, your parents stop receiving school report cards'.
And from then on, they miss out on an important part of their child's adult lives.

Indra was determined to change that.
So, over the course of her career, she wrote 400 handwritten letters to the parents of her -1 and -2 reports.

'Thank you for the gift of your child to PepsiCo. Here's why they're important to us. Here's what they do for others'.

Human.
Simple.
Real.

To this day, those executives, those families, cherish this as one of their fondest memories.

One parent was so overwhelmed with joy, that he made 100 copies of that letter.
And he proudly stood in the hall of his apartment building, waiting for his neighbours to arrive.

He would then hand them a copy and say 'Look - this is what the CEO of PepsiCo said about my son.

'MY son'.
We can be sceptical about Indra's actions.
'What's the ROI of that?'
'How can you measure the impact?'
'How does it impact the bottom line?'

But if for one split second.
You smiled thinking about this gesture.
About someone doing it for you.
Or you doing it for someone else?
Isn't it worth it?

Dear Indra Nooyi - you will probably never read this. If you ever do, please share with us one of those letters.
It's an example for us all.
Our work world needs more of those.

May that letter be the living proof.
That humanity and connection.
Business and work.
Can at times live under the same roof.

And create memories that last a lifetime.

Feeling Overwhelmed Right Now? Try This

Imagine a balloon.
Filled with helium, hanging from your wrist by a thread.
Right above our heads.

The trigger or situation that is causing those racing thoughts.

Take it and put it inside the balloon. Squeeze it in.

Now close your eyes, as hard as you can.
And let the balloon go.

Imagine it going up, up, up in the air.
Floating, floating… until it disappears into the sky.

If those racing thoughts still persist, try this 2 or 3 times.
This brings me balance and peace.

I hope it does the same for you too.

How Southwest Airlines Turned-Around

140 dollars.
That's how much cash this airline had in the bank in 1972.
Not enough to pay a pilot's salary for the day, let alone operate a whole fleet.

So, how did they avoid going down fast?
I decided to play detective and find the secret...
Here's what I found:

Bleeding cash, Southwest Airlines had to sell 1 of its 4 planes to survive. Which meant they would need to run the same number of routes... with 1 less plane.

After doing the math, there was only one option: reduce the time it took for planes to be ready from landing to take-off... to 10 minutes.

10 minutes.

This turn-around time seemed crazy, compared to the industry average of 45 minutes. A seemingly Herculean task.

Instead of giving up, pilots, engineers, stewards, maintenance and managers brought their heads together to devise a near-impossible solution.

One engineer suggested looking outside the industry:
'Should we look at how Formula one cars do their pit stops so fast?'
So, they did. They started to look at how to shave off even a few seconds during every tiny operation. Removing rubbish. Unloading bags. Restocking catering. Even retrieving lost items.

As soon as the plane landed, it was like a well-rehearsed dance. Each person knew exactly what to do. With a total of 100 steps for the turn-around, every second mattered.

Pilots and stewards would take hand luggage out, help clean and even restock peanuts. Nothing was beneath them.

Ground crew would load/off-load baggage... at the same time.
Gate crew would have all passengers lined up and ready to board.
Maintenance would rehearse beforehand and deliver flawlessly.
Even passengers helped by finding a seat during the taxi out.

Through a collective effort, the Southwest Airlines 10-minute-turn was achieved. 100 steps completed in 10 minutes. I take longer than that to iron a shirt*

In 1973, Southwest Airlines turned profitable for the first time.

In 2022, despite tighter security rules, Southwest still is the benchmark for turn-around time in aviation.

Out of crisis, working together became the norm.
Out of scarcity, looking outside became imperative.
Out of need, creativity led to survival.

*Even after 10 minutes of ironing, my shirt has the exact same number of creases.

If Only

If only we remembered to look down as often as we look up.
If only we paused before thinking about the next big thing.
If only we realized that where we are is perfect enough.
If only we accepted imperfection to be the summit.
If only we did all of these, just once in our lives.
If only, just for today. Starting today.
If only, just for a moment.
If only, just now.
If only.

Toxic Positivity

Toxic positivity spreads like wildfire.
The antidote?

Being real, without delay.

If it's good, say it.
If it's bad, say it.
If you don't know, say it.

Nice And Kind Are Not The Same

2009, Australia Grand Slam. Nadal had just won against the legend: Federer.
His victory speech was unexpected.

At the end of the game, and after a streak of bad results, Federer was devastated.

So much so that, when he went to give his concession speech, he broke down crying.

"God, this is killing me", after which he started sobbing and had to stop talking.

When he went up on the podium, Nadal picked up the microphone and said: "Roger, I'm sorry for today."

The audience laughed, not knowing what was going on.

Rafa continued, "I really know how you feel right now, it's tough. But remember, you are a champion, the best in history. I wish you the best of luck for the season."

'What the hell,' I thought when I heard it.

Nadal had won, fair and square.
Against the greatest player of all time.
So why would he apologize?
Why would he care about it?

Why was he being weak?
Then I understood.
Rafa wasn't weak.
He wasn't nice.

He was kind.

I used to confuse kindness with weakness. With niceness.

Because is it harder to be kind... or to do nothing? Doesn't it take more thoughtfulness? Isn't it a sign of strength?

Rafa showed us that we can do the right thing for ourselves. Without crushing others.

That you can empathize with others. Without absorbing their feelings.

That when you have power, you can raise others. Instead of putting them down.

We can live in a world of winners vs losers.
Of champions vs seconds.
Of givers vs takers.

Or we can live in a world where.
Regardless if we win or if we lose.
We leave a mark... by treating others right.

Weakness is temporary.
Niceness is ephemeral.
Kindness lasts forever.

On Being Real

The difference between being real and being 'authentic'?
For those who write, being real feels clumsy, raw, and unpolished.

But for those who read...
Being real feels more soothing, more natural, more human.

Mute that impostor syndrome voice in your head.

Write as you feel.
Speak as you like.
We are all eyes and ears.

Soft Is The New Strong

1. That pain in your chest right before you apologise to someone?

How unpleasant is that compared to keeping your pride and doing nothing?

2. That dryness in your mouth when you say in front of your whole team 'I don't know'?

How uncomfortable is that compared to (pretending) to have all the answers?

3. That knot in your stomach when you give constructive, real feedback?

How uneasy is that compared to saying nothing or resorting to criticism?

4. The shakiness in your breath when someone asks if you're ok, and you're about to burst into tears?

How painful is that compared to just sticking it out and talking business?

5. That sinking feeling right before admitting to yourself and your team that you need to rest?

How awkward is that compared to stoically keeping going until you burn out?

Doing each of these 5 things is often called 'being soft'.
Instead of what we call being 'tough' or 'strong'.

But think about what we feel in each one of these 5 moments.
Don't these actions take way more strength and resolve?

It's time to reframe what 'being soft' means.
Maybe we all need to role model and praise 'soft' examples.
Even if others think that… 'we're just being soft'.

Because maybe, just maybe.
Soft is the New Strong.

Arrivals And Departures

Gates 1-36   About 5-15 minutes   Gates 40-80   About 10-12 m   About 20-25 M

A simple, random act of kindness.
Half selfless, half selfish.
At least that's what it seemed...

"Here's this book for you. I bought the same one for me. We are going to read it at the same time", she said.

I appreciated the gesture, but I was confused.
Why had she bought the exact same book for herself?

"Your copy is to help you go through your journey".
My copy is to help me understand what you're going through. So I can help".

A simple act of kindness.

Throughout the years, she showed me this was not a random act.

By how she was there for me, when I was at my worst.
Or how she laughed when life threw us lemons.
How she supported her family, unconditionally.
And how she pushed us, and herself, to grow.

That day, in that moment, with that book.
That's how Renay arrived in my life.
With a splash.

That splash turned strangers into friends.
Friends into loving partners.
Parting partners into friends.

But still co-parents of the best dog in the world - Lulu.
(Important to clarify - woof woof - Lulu approves this message).

See, life is full of Arrivals and Departures.
Both can make us laugh or cry.
Be content or hurt.
Be happy or sad.

But even in the midst of gutting feelings of loss.
Choosing to be kind is a win for everyone.

And that's what I will remember her for.
For that "random" action, on that day.
For kindness.
For love.
For life.

Mental Health Is... Health

One day, I hope Mental (Health) Education will be taught at every school.

As common as Math, PE, or Geography.

And my kids' report cards will look like this:
Math: B Physical Education: A- Mental Education: A
Geography: D

Because if they take after me, poor kids will suck at geography.

The Idea That Changed VIMEO's History

VIMEO was being badly beaten,
unable to compete with giants.

But in 2014, young Anjali Sud joined as director of marketing.
She had an idea that would forever change Vimeo's history.

Noticing how giants like YouTube and Netflix were investing billions in content, she thought:
'What if we change our focus to help small content creators and businesses to make videos?"
But she was 'just' the 31-year-old director of marketing:
'How can I propose changing the course of the entire company?'

Still, she brushed her doubts off and pitched it to the CEO, Joey Levin.

He thought it was too much of a crazy idea.
But he liked to throw young talent into the deep end.
He said: "I'll carve out a team of 50 people and you're off on your own - you have 1 year to prove this works. Run with it."
He let her loose.

3 years later, that idea took Anjali Sud to the status of CEO.
7 years later, VIMEO is close to 400 billion US$ in sales, 4x their 2014 revenue.

Anjali did a remarkable job, and her story has been told multiple times.
We will never know what Joey Levin did to help her, besides giving her a team. But I can try to guess:

He shielded her from the politics and the naysayers.
He prevented her from having to align every move with 17 people.
He didn't ask for daily reports or status updates.
He didn't ask her to break even in one month.
He let her loose.

Anjali, her 50 strong-team and 1 champion - Joey.
That's all it took to change the course of a whole company.

An inspiration to us, whether we are in a small or big company.

A silent call-to-action for us to:
Be like Anjali, and take the plunge for what we believe in.
Be like Anjali's team, breaking barriers with passion and grit.
Be like Joey, letting them loose.

But what if they fail, you might ask?
They will be happy because they tried.
And what if they succeed?
They can rewrite history.
Like Anjali Sud did.

So let them loose.
What do you have to lose?

Being Kind At Work

Is being kind at work the same as being soft or fragile?

That's how most of us were brought up, but it's way harder to be kind than to be tough... or do nothing.
It takes more thought and intention.
It's a sign of being strong, not weak or fragile.

Being kind can be the foundation for a culture that makes our days easier, more joyful and balanced.

Kindness is concrete. And easier to put into practice when we see it in action at work.

5 examples of kindness I recently witnessed:

- Treating suppliers and partners as if you have no power over them. You'll be on the other side one day, and you'll want to be treated equally.

- Explaining the big picture of what you're trying to achieve to every person, not only to those who have power. We are all looking for purpose, for something bigger than ourselves.

- Giving your time to someone that has nothing to offer you in return. I bet you recall at least 10 people that have done that for you. In fact - take the time today to thank one of those people, message them, call them.

- Going out of your way to make someone smile or listen to them cry. Or smile and cry together. They will remember that for years.

- Checking in with someone for no clear reason - even if you're super busy. Because "everyone you meet is fighting a battle you know nothing about. Be kind, always."

I fail often but try to do one act of kindness per day. And this includes me - as we tend to unleash the Kraken on ourselves and be our fiercest critics.

Highlighting good examples of kindness is what will propel our work cultures forward.

We Aren't Tired Of A 'Corporate' World

We just got distracted.

We forgot the true meaning of corporate words. So bringing that back is about finding concrete examples.
Turning words into principles, principles into actions, and actions into human connections.

To make our workplaces more human, we can try to replace:

Authenticity with… Realness
Teamwork with… Comradery
Seriousness with… Laughter
Feedback with… Care
Culture with… Behaviours
Psychological Safety with… Comfort
Politics with… Data
Strategy with… Direction
Networking with… Relationships
Being vulnerable with… Being Human.

I am unable to do these 10 things at all times.
But every day, I pick one and try to put it into action.

Instead of ditching the corporate world…
Let's try to make it more human first.

7 Ideas When Starting A New Job

1. Forget about all of this Game-of-Thrones-stakeholder mapping stuff. Talk with as many people as you can. Internal, external, senior, not-so-senior, new-hire or long-timer.

Perspective is priceless.

2. Read *The Culture Map* by Erin Meyer. It taught me how to understand others based on their background and context. And never to make assumptions about anything. As a good friend says:

Assumptions are the mother of all screw-ups.

3. There will be this annoying voice in your head - 'You're gonna fail, it is NOW that you're gonna be found out'. When this happens, read your offer letter aloud. You got it for a reason.

Tons of people believed in you.
Time for you to do the same.

4. Ask questions and listen. Just listen. I know this voice in our head says that we SHOULD add value from the outset. But no one really ever does that. If they try, 8 out of 10 times they screw up.
Have you ever heard anyone say 'Great addition to the team, but I think he/she listens too much'?

5. Have a plan, not about HOW but WHAT you want to achieve. 'Strategy is just a sense of direction around which you can improvise ' (Peter Drucker). Knowing the WHAT grounds you, and shows others the direction, even if the HOW needs to change at some point.

In a deck, in a doc, in Miro, on a napkin. Just have a plan.

6. Treat the 'powerful' people like the humans they are. They have a different title but want the same things as us. Being heard, having an impact and working for a greater purpose.

If you treat them equally they will do the same.
If they don't, you still did the right thing.

7. Bring your freshness of thinking, your ideas. That's the best way to help yourself and the team you joined. It may bring them some anxiety, but they hired you for that.

And if they don't welcome your ideas, you probably shouldn't hang around for long.

Try This

Next time you have an Innovation board, Executive review or <insert fancy name> Committee, bring with you the most (seemingly) junior person on your team.

Let them voice their opinion on every topic. Don't interrupt, just listen. And see what happens.

Innovation is a process, not an outcome.

"You Have Gaps On Your CV"

The next time someone asks you.
'Can you explain this gap on your CV?'
Or 'what made you change jobs'?
Tell them this story.

He was performing at his highest level.
Winning a ton of awards.
Then he decided he had enough.
So he took a break.

Then moved to a totally different job.
Did it for 1 year. Didn't love it.
So he went back to his old job.
When asked why, he said:
'I'm back'.

Michael Jordan.
From basketball to baseball.
And back.
From a winning streak to a break.
And back.

He became The Greatest of All Time.
Because of all of this.
Not in spite of it.

It's time to let go of misconceptions at work:
That change with intent is 'job-hopping'.
That slowing down = you're not committed.
That progress is only linear + straight up.
That resting is a 'gap', instead of a break.

Because my dear friends,
if the Greatest of All time needed a break.
Why wouldn't we, common mortals?

The Berlin Bottle Man

A friend asked me: 'Why do you write more about others, than about yourself?'
So I told him the story of Claus.
The Berlin Bottle man.

Claus is a 56-year-old manager by day.
An amateur triathlete by night.
But he's so much more than that.

He has volunteered at the Berlin marathon since 1998. In the 2022 edition, he had one job. To handover water bottles to Eliud Kipchoge, the world record holder.

Simple, easy, one would think.
But Claus takes this little task.
And makes it special.

To ensure the perfect handover, he practices with a tulip inside a vase. A frickin' tulip.

Before handing a bottle, he stares at Eliud while shouting his name out loud.

When he handles it, he high-fives himself with such joy and energy.

And then he quickly hops on his bike to sprint to the next handover.

The result: in last week's Berlin marathon, Eliud broke his own world marathon record.

His first one had been established in 2018.
Guess who delivered him bottles then?
Claus. Here's what Eliud said then:

'My biggest remembrance of Berlin is the guy who was handing me water, still my hero up to now. The way he was handling and acting and talking was unbelievable'.

Now, I can be sceptical and think Claus has a minor role.
That anyone could do it.
That the merit is on the runner.

But is this really true? Aren't big things made... of a thousand little things?

Small cheers.
Gentle pushes.
Or just being there.

When we put care and love into little things.
They add up to the biggest things of all.
From small victories to world records.

That's why I write about others.
Because with their help and support.
Whether I'm crawling, walking or running.

I go a little faster.
Feel a little better.
Push a little harder.

They are the heroes.
Not me.
So I'll keep writing about the 'Claus' in my life.

Because they've always been there for me.
And they probably will always be.

What Lasts A Lifetime?

In 10 years you won't remember revenues, budgets, titles or projects.

But you will be remembered by how you felt - and how you made others feel.

WHAT you get is short-lived.

HOW you got it lasts a lifetime.

The Little Things

We know how a toxic work environment feels like.
The triggers, the behaviours, and the impact.
But what's the big secret of a great work environment?

It's... the little things.

It's the big group laughter when one of us cracks a joke.
It's the burst of energy you feel, the day before seeing your colleagues in person.
It's being recognized not by what you achieved, but by how you got there.

It's... the little things.

It's sharing personal moments, as they're part of who we are.
It's being told the truth, even when it's hard and hurts like hell.
It's not craving to claim credit, because in the end we all win.

It's... the little things.

It's knowing we have each other's backs, without having to say it out loud.
It's taking the blame as a team, despite it probably being solely my fault.
It's asking ourselves 'I actually get paid to work with these people every day?'

It's... the little things.

It's chatting because we want to, not only if we have an agenda.
It's wanting to tell our family about how our work day went.
It's making stories that we know we'll remember for years.

It's... the little things.

It's feeling like a group of friends, with boundaries that don't need spelling out.
It's smiling when you think about random moments at work.
It's secretly hoping that things will never change.

Is it values? Is it behaviour?
Is it the norm? Is it people?

I'm not sure what it is.
Maybe it's a mix of it all.
But it certainly is... no little thing.

If You Broke A Leg...

Would you say any of these 5 things to yourself?

1. 'I can't tell anyone, they'll think I'm weak.'
2. 'I'm just gonna get on with it, I'll be fine.'
3. 'I have a perfect life, how could this happen to me?'
4. 'I'll be fine after a couple of physio sessions.'
5. 'I don't need rest, back to running tomorrow!'

You probably wouldn't.

If you wouldn't say these things for a physical injury...
Why would you if you were going through a period of poor mental health?

A mental health issue can be much more dangerous than a physical injury. But with an injury, at least those around you can see it, and know what you're going through.
And you know the exact steps it takes to recover.

We recognize a broken leg.
We can feel the pain, see the swelling, spot the bruising.
We know exactly what to do to heal.

This isn't the case with mental illness.

We are still learning how to talk about it and deal with it.

We can bust the stigma by doing these 5 things instead:

1. Not being ashamed of sharing the burden with others.
2. Learning to recognize the symptoms in ourselves and slowing down before we crash.
3. Knowing that everyone needs help sometimes, regardless of how 'perfect' their life seems to be.
4. Accepting the time and steps it takes to recover.
5. Resting until you heal. "If you get tired learn to rest, not to quit" – Banksy.

So, if you read this today, and find yourself going through a mental health challenge.
Say to yourself what you would say to a close friend:

'Rest and recover. Take your time to heal.
Come back when and if you feel ready.'
Even if you don't believe it yet, say it aloud.
If you can't do it yet, that's ok - say it to others.

And maybe one day...
Mental health won't be 'a thing' anymore.
It will just be like... a broken leg.

No One Has It Figured Out

All the frickin' time.
Every one of us:

Thinks 'this happy moment' will be followed by tragedy.
Trusts more in others' abilities than in ourselves.
Feels they're 'gonna be found out' one day.
Fears they're gonna end up alone.
Doubts themselves so often.
Feels like crap some days.
Is scared beyond belief.

Every. One. Of. Us.

We just don't see it.
Because we ourselves.
Don't let others see it. Do we?
So here I am. Naked (a figure of speech!).
Telling you that I don't have it all figured out.
Because... I don't have to. All the frickin time.

Neither. Do. You.

"I'm Toast"

18 minutes into the interview.

I was gone. I was toast.

After 6 interviews, this was the last one.
There I was in front of Paco Ballesters.

These thoughts going through my mind.

'Why is he asking questions back, didn't he like my answer?'
'Why does he ask about my opinions, not my experience?'
'How come he is so quiet when I speak?'

Then he said what I thought was the final blow.
'Marco, we ran out of time'.
I knew it. 'You're an idiot'.
I said to myself.

The. Stories. We. Tell. Ourselves.

But then Paco continued:
'But I'm enjoying this conversation.
So I would like to continue talking to you'.

It was only months later that I understood.
That this is what made Paco the leader we followed.

He was not interested in my achievements, but in my values.
He was not interested in what I had done, but what I could do.
He was not interested in interrogating me, to prove he was strong.

He saw me… he saw us for what we were.
Not for what we had achieved.
But how we got there.

That's what makes him a leader.
We will remember for life.

The. Stories. We. Tell. Ourselves.

Before that moment, I couldn't imagine a different ending.
But there always are 100 possible endings.

And it might just not be the end.

It might be a new chapter to be told.
A new paragraph to be written.
Or it just might be a moment.
Waiting to unfold.

The. Stories. We. Tell. Ourselves.

"The Mean CFO"

"Don't even go and speak with him, he's the enemy".

"He just sees numbers. The typical CFO," they added.

That's what someone said to me.
Before I met Freddy Lepiz for the first time.

In a surprising turn of events. I spoke with him anyway.
And here's what I found about Freddy.

That he would treat you exactly with the same respect.
Whether you were junior or senior, insider or outsider.

That he would first listen to understand your opinion.
Even if he had seen that situation a 100 times before.

That numbers wouldn't rule his opinions.
But values, principles would.

That his role is not what defines him.
But his kindness, his humour, his compassion, his grace.

As for the person that had given me that advice.
It would not be fair for me to call him an idiot.
It was his truth, what he believed in.

That doesn't mean he was right.
Had I not acted on what I believed, being curious.
I would've missed out, on one of the best humans I met in my career.

So, thank you, Freddy.
For being one of those Imperfect Heroes.
That are all around us. That teach us to be better.

Freddy, I will always remember you, 'the mean" CFO.
When I asked you at the end of a tough meeting.
'Are you happy, Freddy? You would simply reply with.

"Are you happy? If you're happy, I'm happy"

Not bad for an "enemy".
Not bad, Freddy.
My dear friend.

Help And Mental Health

It was only after my own experiences with mental health.
That I realized how much I screwed up.
When I 'tried to help' someone.

But I try not to give myself a hard time for that.
I didn't grow up discussing 'mental health'.
I would either not hear anything about it.
Or listen to 'People are sometimes sad'.

But now I can do something about it.
In the middle of depression, anxiety.
The right gesture, a kind word.
Can make a big difference.
Even if for one day.

Here are 3 things I do differently today to try to help:

Instead of claiming 'You're too hard on yourself.'
I say 'What would you say to a close friend?'
Giving perspective, not advice.

Instead of asking 'Do you want to talk about it?'
I stay in silence… and let them lead.
They will speak when and if they want.

Instead of saying 'You will be ok'.
I say 'I'm here for you today'.
It's okay not being okay.

One single day of being there, helping out.
May be worth a lifetime for others.

Fear Of Failure

Fear of failure. It's always there.
I used to fight it. I still do.
But now…

I pull up a magic wand.
I turn fear into insecurity.
Insecurity grounds me.
Prepares me.

Insecurity can be a blessing.
Make us work harder, better.
And take us to those very places.
That fear itself never thought we would get to one day.

"What If..."?

How much time, energy would we save in our lives.
By more often asking the question.
That he asked me that day.

Wahib Sbai was my recruiter during an interview process.
After the 3rd chat back and forth, he asked me:

'What if we hop on a call and sort it out together?'
As simple, as easy, as human as that.
And he didn't stop there.

He was clear when there was complexity.
He was kind when there was ambiguity.
He was real when there was anxiety.

See, sometimes we blame it on 'the system'.
'That's just how things work around here.'
But there's no such thing as corporate.
Corporate is people. Corporate is us.

So thank you Wahib. For being an Imperfect Hero.
Humans like you are what makes corporate.
What it really should and can be.
More human. More... us.

Labels

I used to put labels on people.
I still do sometimes.
Even when I don't even know them.

And oh boy, did I put a big label on Moez Youssef.

Before I got to know him, the label was: the "Ethics & Compliance" guy that's here only to slow us down.

After coffee chats and long conversations, that label exploded in my face like an overheated marshmallow.

I found out he was a caring, incredibly aware human, that enables others to move faster and surely.

I found out that he has an impressive collection of shoes. Including 4 different Air Jordans. BAM!

I found out that listening to the waves soothes him. It brings him to where he grew up, by the sea.

I found out that others see him as a beacon of kindness, calm, humour and professionalism.

I found out that he's like most of us.
Aware of his flaws, humble of his legacy.
An unfinished business, an imperfect human.
But a pretty good one, as unbiasedly judged by... me.

So yeah, labels are there for a reason.
Even if that reason is for us... to peel them off.

And seeing people for what they are.
Seeing the humans behind the roles.
Seeing people behind the pros.
Seeing... them.

I see you Moez, my dear friend.
I see you. And your cool Air Jordans.

What Is Company Culture After All

Culture is about the behaviors we witness being rewarded.

It's not about the bold statements of intent.

Or the 5-pillar multi-year initiatives.

It's about... them.

It's praising them not only for what they achieved.
But how they got there.

It's highlighting them for telling the truth.
Even when it's hard and hurts like hell.

It's rewarding them for the right things.

For behaviors over outcomes.
For values over statements.
For people over processes.
For actions over words.

7327 Days

7327 days.

No wonder I lost our bet.

Every time I went for coffee with her.

One day, my friend Ana Flores left Novartis for a new adventure. After 7327 days. 20 years and counting.

We had only worked 365 days together. I thought we would remember our fancy projects and our business wins.

Instead, I remember our laughs at the cafeteria.

Coffee with Ana was a challenge. With her great reputation, every 2 mins someone would wave at her.

We made a bet: to count how many times we would wave to someone. Whoever lost, would buy coffee.

Well, my coffee bill went through the roof. It became so bad, that I started 'fake-waving' at people.

Why did so many wave at her? I don't know.

Maybe because she chose to be curious, open. Instead of staying with "But we've done like this for 20 years".

Or because she always looked out for her people.
Before looking out for herself.

Or because she chose to do the hard work to grow.
By choosing to change her first. Not others.

I don't know.
But this… I do know.

I miss my friend Ana.

Being Goofy

It's possible to be goofy at times, professional always.
Even if we were taught 'we're not supposed to'.
It is possible to:

Smile and make smile, even if no one is looking.
Be childish in a grown-up mind and body.
Crack jokes while still being respectful.
Laugh in the face of misery.
Diffuse stress with humour.
Replace gravity with levity.

I know it's hard, we're conditioned to think otherwise.
So everyday I fight for it, try to do it.

95% of the time, the outcome is good.
5% of the time is bad in some way.

But even when it turns out bad.
It's not that bad, anyway.

Because it makes me feel more human, more me.
And it might, it just might make someone else.
Feel a tiny wee bit more human too.

Even if 'we're not supposed to'.

Even for a goofy moment.
Even for a short laugh.
Even for a brief smile.

The Character I Want To Be

I can't choose how others will react.
But I can choose how I will.

I can't choose what I'm faced with.
But I can choose what I stand for.

I can't choose the battles that come my way.
But I can choose the ones worth fighting.

I can't choose how others speak to me.
But I can choose how kindly I talk to myself.

I can't choose the outcomes of what I do.
But I can choose how I show up when I do it.

I can't choose who feels threatened by me.
But I can choose the boundaries I set.

I can't choose how the story ends.
But I can choose the character I want to be.

I can choose.
I can choose.

I. Can. Choose.

She Only Had 1 Follower

She has 24k followers today.
But when she was 7 years old.
She only had one.

Back then she made a promise to herself.
One day she would be heard.
She would have a voice.

She started performing for her family.
Then on every stage she could find.
Now she performs for the world.

She could have settled for that.
Pure, stand-alone achievement.

But no. She made a conscious decision.

"I will give others the help I wish I had gotten when I was 7"
I will shine… because I made them shine".
And she did.

With all these followers, talent and reputation.
You would think that grown-up Nausheen I. Chen:

Always believes in herself.
Always has an answer. Always is at her best.
Always feels she's not disappointing others.

Never feels she's gonna be found out.
Never has doubts. Never feels weak.
Never needs to rest.

But oh boy, she does.
Every. Single. Day.

But she pushes through.
When she's unable to write, she rests.
When she's not at her best, she still shows up.
When she has her doubts, she helps others with theirs.

See, we don't follow people because they don't fall.
We follow people because they fall…
And get back up again.
And again. And again.

That's why we will continue to follow your journey, Nausheen.
Your Imperfect Story.

With your signature purple hair.
With your wisdom, kindness and wit.

From that one follower who dared to believe in herself.
To thousands of followers that will continue to believe in you.

Every. Single. Day.

Perspective Is Everything

I'm weak, not kind.

So don't try to convince me that.
My kindness means strength.

Because at the end of the day
There is no value in acting that way.

And I'm not going to lie to myself by thinking
Kindness is how I should treat others.

So rest assured that I know
It's ok to stop being kind.

And nothing you say will make me think
I should be proud to act with kindness.

Because as every good, kind human
I cannot stand on my own.

And because of that I simply can't believe
Being kind means being strong.

(Now read this again from the bottom to the top).

Perspective is everything.

Being kind is my choice.
Mistaking it for weakness was yours.

How I Manage Thoughts

Words are always real.
Thoughts sometimes are not.
So how do I manage my thoughts?

See, my brain sometimes lies to me.
Tells me things that aren't true.
Fires thoughts that aren't so.

So I throw words at those thoughts.
I say them out loud.
I write them down.

I tell my thoughts what they don't want to hear.
I fight them back with different perspectives.
Then thoughts are screwed.

Because they can't throw words back at me.
So they become what they are.
'They're just thoughts'.

Just uttering these 3 simple words.
Scares the crap out of them.
So they go away.
And words…
They stay.

'They're just thoughts'.

The Story Of Gabriella

I couldn't believe she asked me that.
As we came out of an external presentation:
'Marco, did you also feel dumb looking at those slides?'

We both burst out laughing.

3 graphs per slide, topped by abundant jargon.
She said exactly what I was thinking the entire time.
But I wasn't strong enough to admit or joke about it.

That was my first glimpse into Gabriella Messinese.
Since then, I learned so much more about who she is:

Challenging not the outcomes, but the values that guide our decisions.

Finding 7 solutions for a problem, instead of 14 reasons why it cannot be solved.

Building bridges between people, tearing down walls while she's at it.

Choosing to be curious instead of fearful, joyful instead of dull.

Leading with laughter over misery. Showing over telling. Doing over preaching (can I get a Hallelujah!)

So thank you, Gabriella.
For being one of those Imperfect Heroes.
Who are all around us.

That inspire us. That we learn from.
That teach us to be better.

You're someone I would go to any battle with.
Someone I can laugh and cry with.

And most importantly, someone...
I would trust my dog with.

First things first, people!

First things first. Woof-woof.

20 Things I Wish I Knew

20 things I wish I knew when I was in my 20's:

Tiramisu is the best dessert in the world.
Matching your dog's outfit is SO COOL.
Happiness is moments of contentment.
Don't grow a ponytail in your teens.
Laughter makes life more bearable.
Everyone has a voice in their head.
Life is better with GIF's & memes.
Toxic people are never worth it.
I remember people, not things.
When they go low, I go high.
I love it, change it or leave it.
Kindness is not weakness.
No one has it figured out.
No one reads pre-reads.
When I'm tired, I... rest.
Ewoks are NOT bears.
Dogs are awesome.
Writing posts.
That look like.
Stairs is very.
Hard to.
Do.

What They Taught Me

"But why do you help people?".
I do it because of them.
What they taught ME.

I met Bruno Sampaio dos Reis and Nerea Rosell Uriz
15 years ago, when I was looking for a job.

They had no reason to believe in me.
I had no experience. No "big brands". No network.

It was just ME.
Yet, they believed in ME.

Bruno believed in a kid who wanted to study management. Even if I had never done it before.
So he referred me to Esade Business School.

Nerea believed in a kid that wanted to learn his passion - marketing in the best school in the world.
She referred me to Procter & Gamble.

Those small gestures from THEM.
These 2 Imperfect Heroes.
Meant huge leaps for ME.

And they also provided after-sales service.
Kept the faith in me when I had lost it myself.
Had patience for me, when I was impatient.
Mentored me, with kindness and care.

That's why 15 years from now, 2 things will still be true:
- They still haven't aged at all (not that I am jealous).
- We will continue to be friends for a lifetime.

So yeah. I'm helping. Everyday.
Because they taught me this one thing:

"If you're looking for a job, today, I will help you.
Because I've been there... where you are today.

And I'll be there again... where you are today

One day."

What Good Leaders Did For Me

I don't know what a leader is supposed to do.
In times of chaos and uncertainty.
Here's what good leaders did for me:

They helped me help us focus on what I could control. And park what I couldn't at that point in time.

They told me "It's ok not to be ok". More important, they role-modeled it, and walked the talk every day.

They remarked that as important as our jobs were, personal balance always came first. Period.

They reminded me I was not a neurosurgeon. That if at times I didn't give 100% at work, no one would die**

Leadership...
It's not a position.
It's not a status.

It's an attitude.

**(If you're a neurosurgeon, I accept that this story won't resonate)

Tell Me More

7.63 minutes into our intro chit-chat.

Things took an unexpected turn.

Me and Isabel Afonso were meeting for the first time.
"The usual intro with a senior leader", I thought.

Then we started talking about Chat GPT.
That's when she told me these 3 magic words:

"Tell. Me. More"

To which I answered:
"What if I show you?".

We sprinted out of that meeting room to get my laptop.
And spent the time playing with Chat-GPT.

Isabel spent the weeks after reading avidly about it.
But why?

Why did she care in the midst of barcode calendars, strategy meetings and business plans?

My hypothesis is: we're past the era of the stoic leader.
The "know-it-all". The "I-always-I-have-answers"

The world is moving too fast for that to work.

It's about taking an interest in people.
Regardless of how junior or seasoned they are.

It's about how curious you stay.
Regardless of how experienced you are.

It's about the questions you ask.
Regardless of the answers you have.

That's the 21st-century leader.

That's who Isabel is.

She didn't tell me that's who she was.
She showed me. With 3 words.

"Tell. Me. More"

On Feeling Regret

Feeling regret is scarier than taking the first step.

Yes I might fall.
Even heroes do.
That's not what defines them.

What does is: they get back up again.

And again.
And again.
And again.

I push through temporary fear, today.
So I don't have a lifetime of regret, tomorrow.

But yeah sometimes I'm scared.
As scared as a snowman in a sauna.
(I clearly have lived in Switzerland for too long).

Mental Health At Work

Managing Mental Health at work.

It's easy-peasy.

Just do what I do.

I only do tasks that energize me.
I check e-mail every 2 days for 5 minutes.
I have total control over my scope of work.
I never work with people I don't like or agree with.
I have a perfect diary, with plenty of time for myself.

Not really. No one does this.
Here's what I really do:
When I'm energized I work, full-on. When I'm tired I rest, without feeling guilty.

I do whatever task is needed. As long as it doesn't compromise my values. The moral injury is not worth it.

I work with everyone, but I balance what I need with what they want. And I expect them to do the same.

I get out for fresh air. 5 minutes make all the difference. Walking 1:1's work wonders.

I don't over-engineer mindfulness. It can be driving, listening to music, breathing for 30 seconds.

I make mental and physical health part of my diary.
It helps me and it helps others.

Most importantly - I talk about mental health.
It's not "a thing". It's just part of who we are.

At home, at work. In life.

Today I can brag that I dead-lifted 135kg at the gym**
One day I'll brag about doing therapy once a week.

Word.
** Never have I ever lifted that. Never will I ever.

Just Take An Interest

At the end of my "wacky" presentation.

He came and asked me one simple question.

"Hey I loved your presentation and crazy ideas!
Can we chat more about it?"

I thought Martin Peters was just being kind.
But why would he even bother to do that?
I had no pedigree, no seniority. No Pharma experience.

Well... he was taking an interest in me.
Instead of being comfortable with what he knew.
He wanted to find out what he didn't know.

That simple moment of interest allowed me to lift the veil. Of who Martin is and how he rolls.

He has the knowledge to give answers.
But prefers to ask questions instead.

He has the brain to add complexity.
But leads with clarity and simplicity.

He has the experience to tell us what will fail.
But chooses to build over tearing apart.

He has the gravitas to command a room.
But instead chooses to spotlight others.

We overdo and overthink things in corporate.
We call it stakeholder engagement.
We call it "generating rapport".
We call it networking.

It's much, much simpler than that.
It starts by taking an interest.
By being human.

Just like Martin did.

Who You Gonna Call?

In the 80's we called The Ghostbusters.

In the 2020's, "who you gonna call?"

Well, I call Mamoudou Wane.
I was driving an innovation project, close to giving up.
Lost in a maze of people and technical requirements.

When we met, I can imagine his first thought:

"Another guy with crazy ideas, that will never fly in Pharma. Let me throw a smoke bomb and RUN FORREST, RUN!"

If that was his first thought… he didn't act on it.
He took an interest. He asked questions.

Because that's just who he is. The (legal version) of Mr Wolf from Pulp Fiction.

Keeping calm, cool and collected.
Like a Buddhist monk meditating next to a volcano.

De-escalating and simplifying problems. With a smile and witty jokes.

Connecting the dots between people and technology.
Like a maestro bringing together a majestic symphony.

Choosing curiosity over resistance. Possibility over challenge. Future over past.

So thank you Mamoudou.
For being one of those Imperfect Heroes.
Who are all around us.

I'll always gonna call you, my friend.
Regardless of what I have ahead.
Regardless where we both are.

Does Failing Define Us?

My friend Tasleem Ahmad Fateh has 60k followers and makes thousands of dollars every month on LinkedIn.

But this isn't the story I want to share about him.

At the peak of his content creation journey he disappeared from LinkedIn for 3 months.

Why?

He developed an obsessive-compulsive disorder.
Which made him literally pull his beard out.

His courage to come out and say what happened.
Is what I found most impressive.

It made me rethink everything.
About him and those like him.

The "they have it all figured out" ones.
The "successful and bulletproof".
After all, they are just like me. Like us.

Despite their followers, their craft, their art.
They are just everyday humans.
Who fall, hard and often.

So why do we say "The higher they climb, the hardest they fall"?
Because that's what we were taught.

I disagree.

Falling doesn't define us.
How we bounce back does.

The stronger they bounce back.
The higher they climb on my list.

Those are the real Heroes.

Not the flawless ones.
But the Imperfect ones.
And you Tasleem, are one of them.

How LEGO Came Back Into My Life

The untold story of how LEGO came back into my life.

The eve of what would be one of my worst days.

2018, a few days before May the 4th.
I was walking through central London.
A feeling made me enter Hamley's, a toy store.

The LEGO Millenium Falcon was on display.
The biggest Lego set ever made, 7500 bricks baby!
Stocked out everywhere, going for 3x retail on eBay.

With 1% hope, I asked the store clerk if it was in stock.
He answered: "It's your lucky day! We just had a return, this is the last box in all of London".

I couldn't believe it. I hadn't bought LEGO in 20 years. But I was afraid of the next day.

So I asked him to reserve it for 2 hours. And went for dinner with my friend Gabriel Lacerda.

I asked him: "What if I buy it and the worst happens? Won't I be defying karma?"

His answer was annoyingly simple and wise, as always.

"Do you deserve it? Yes. Can you afford it? Yes."

"If you have good news, you celebrate by building it"
"If the worst happens, you cope by building it."

I went back and bought it.
The worst happened the next day.

I spent the weekend binge-building.
Through the pain, the sorrow.

The incredulity. The crying.
I just kept on building.

And on Sunday, I wrote a plan on a piece of paper.
With 7 mini-plans, all with Star Wars names.

I stored it in my half-built Millenium Falcon.
Where it stays, till this day.

The plan didn't prevent the grueling months that followed. A story for another day.

But building the Falcon taught me that.
No matter how broken you are.
No matter how chaotic things are.
No matter how long it takes to rebuild.

I can do it.
Step by step.
Brick by brick.

I'm still rebuilding. Maybe for the rest of my life. But aren't we all?

As for what made me enter that toy store that day…

I don't know.
Maybe it was chance.
Maybe it was the Force.

Either way, today and always.
May the 4th be with me.
May the Force be with you.

Printed in Poland
by Amazon Fulfillment
Poland Sp. z o.o., Wrocław
01 September 2023

9ffb5dba-2e97-462b-b80b-c5ca5e32c91eR01